MONSTER HIGH

GREAT SCARRIER REEF

LITTLE, BROWN BOOKS FOR YOUNG READERS

First published in the United States in 2016 by Little, Brown and Company
First published in Great Britain in 2016 by Hodder and Stoughton

1 3 5 7 9 10 8 6 4 2

A CIP catalogue record for this book
is available from the British Library.

ISBN 978-1-51020-040-1

Printed and bound in Great Britain by
Clays Ltd, St Ives plc

The paper and board used in this book are
made from wood from responsible sources.

Little, Brown Books for Young Readers
An imprint of
Hachette Children's Group
Part of Hodder and Stoughton
Carmelite House
50 Victoria Embankment
London EC4Y 0DZ

An Hachette UK Company
www.hachette.co.uk

www.hachettechildrens.co.uk

The Junior Novel

ADAPTED BY
Perdita Finn

BASED ON THE SCREENPLAY WRITTEN BY
Nina Bargiel and Shane Amsterdam

LITTLE, BROWN BOOKS FOR YOUNG READERS
www.lbkids.co.uk

Chapter 1

IN THE SWIM OF THINGS

It was almost summer and the campus lawn was buzzing with freaky, breezy monsters headed to class. Clawdeen Wolf skipped up the front steps with Frankie Stein. They were chattering away about dance practice when they passed Cleo de Nile fixing her hair in front of her open locker.

Cleo, who was Egyptian royalty, was not happy. She made a face in the mirror and sighed. "Sometimes I think I should go full mummy," she said to her friend Abbey Bominable.

Abbey frowned. Very little amused her. "Cleo, yeti have saying: Face is beauty when heart is beauty."

Cleo slammed shut her locker. Inner beauty was the least of her concerns.

Clawdeen smiled as she saw Draculaura holding up a sign in front of the Creepateria. It showed a steak circled in red with a big red line through it. Draculaura may have been a vampire, but that didn't mean she couldn't be a vegetarian—and if she could do it, *everyone* could.

Clawdeen's brother Clawd walked by holding a bone. Draculaura couldn't believe it. Even if he was a werewolf, how could her boyfriend do such a thing? "Clawd!" she exclaimed to get his attention. "Don't put the *eat* in *meat*."

Draculaura pulled a stalk of broccoli out of her pocket and swapped it for the bone. Clawd's face fell, but he nibbled on the green stems dutifully. He tried to swallow, but he really couldn't.

"That's a good boy." Draculaura patted his head comfortingly.

A hiss caught her attention. Toralei Stripe, the werecat, and her catty friends Meowlody and Purrsephone were strolling past. "Daughter of Dracula can't stand the sight of blood," she sneered. "Purrrrrfect."

Meowlody and Purrsephone giggled. Their whiskers twitched.

Lagoona Blue, ever thoughtful, rushed over to Draculaura. "Don't let Toralei get to you. That cat should be declawed."

Lagoona Blue was the kind of ghoul who always stood up for her friends. The daughter of a sea monster from the Great Scarrier Reef, she'd left her underwater home to go to school at Monster High. She was the captain of the swim team, naturally, and her life was going swimmingly too. She'd even patched things up with her boyfriend, Gil, whose parents had been unhappy at first about their freshwater son dating a sea monster.

Clawdeen followed Lagoona and Gil to chemistry class. They really were a cute couple.

In the lab, Clawdeen took out a beaker and some test tubes. Frankie Stein got ready to help her with an experiment. Frankie began carefully pouring liquid into the beaker, but sometimes, when she was nervous or excited, it was hard to control the electricity in her body. She accidentally sent out a sizzling zap through her fingers.

Clawdeen's hair frizzled and stood on end. Yup, she knew her friends, and Frankie was always shocking… literally.

"Here, let me give you a hand," said Frankie, apologetic. She detached her left hand from her wrist, molded the fingers into a claw, and offered it to Clawdeen so she could smooth down her hair.

"Thanks!" said Clawdeen. There was nothing like a hand-brush when you needed one.

And there was nothing like ghoulfriends who knew each other inside and out, who had shared all their secrets with each other, who couldn't imagine that their relationships would ever change.

But everything changes—and sometimes when you least expect it.

Outside in the hallway, Heath and Deuce were bouncing a basketball. Heath hurled it around his back at Deuce. He went to catch it, but it flew out of his hands and hit the wall where there was a poster for the dance recital.

A corner of the poster tore and peeled away.

Sometimes when you least expect trouble, trouble is what happens. Even the best friendships can end up in deep water.

Chapter 2

OUT OF THE BLUE

Toralei was rehearsing for the dance recital with the ghouls in the Vampitheater. On her head was a tiny little beret like a director might wear. Toralei was scowling and clapping her hands. She was taking the upcoming performance very seriously.

"Ghouls! Ghouls! Ghouls!" she shouted, trying to get everyone's attention onstage. Music blared from a coffin-shaped boom box. "We need to be fangtastic at this dance recital! I need…scary!" She struck a pose; her paws flared out like jazz hands. "I need spooky!" She growled and raised her arms over her head like a ghost. "I need fun!" She pounced.

"I need a break!" Clawdeen sighed.

Frankie and Draculaura tried not to laugh.

"Who died and made Toralei boss?" whispered Frankie.

"Headmistress Bloodgood, remember?" Draculaura reminded her. "This better be worth the extra credit."

Toralei turned up the music. She glared at the dancers onstage. They only had one more day before the big performance!

The ghouls began swinging their arms and lifting their knees. They jerked and jounced and jolted. They were awful—and they kind of knew it.

"No, no, no, no, NO!" yowled Toralei. "That's terrible!" She leaped up onstage and began to go through the entire routine—only she was even worse than Frankie and Clawdeen and Draculaura. "It looks

like this," she announced, dancing wilder and wilder. She looked like a cat that had fallen into the bathtub.

"Isn't that what we were doing?" Frankie asked the other ghouls, confused.

"It looks awful," noted Clawdeen, "so…yes?"

"Hey, ghouls!" Lagoona glided into the back of the auditorium to have a look at the rehearsals. "Looking…" She paused, watching Toralei. "*Great?*"

Toralei slammed her hand down on the boom box, and the music stopped.

"Lagoona, come join us," invited Frankie.

Lagoona blushed, her blue face turning a soft shade of violet. "Oh, I couldn't possibly. I'm a swimmer, not a dancer."

"If Lagoona wanted to dance, she should have auditioned. Killer moves like these take practice!" snapped Toralei.

The ghouls glanced at one another. Moves? Was that what they had been doing?

Lagoona waved her hands. "That's okay. The stage is really not my thing."

Pleased, Toralei smiled at Lagoona like a Cheshire cat. "If you want to make yourself useful," she purred, "I do need someone to organize the wrap party. Nothing big. Just decorations, music, and food for, like, the entire school."

Lagoona's aqua eyes widened. "Uh…" She hesitated. But she did want to help out her friends. "No problem."

"Don't mess it up!" Toralei warned. "All right, ghouls, I'll see you tomorrow for…" She flared her fingers in what might have been a dance move. "Opening night!"

The ghouls tried to smile, but they did not feel ready. At all. They gathered up their backpacks to head home, but Frankie stopped. She noticed that Lagoona was staring thoughtfully at the stage. Maybe she really did want to be part of the performance. Maybe they should have included Lagoona, despite what she said.

"Lagoona? Are you coming?" asked Frankie.

"I'll catch up," she answered. She seemed far away, as if she were somewhere completely different than the Vampitheater at Monster High.

When she was certain that all the ghouls had left, Lagoona walked up onstage in the empty theater. She looked around one more time to make sure she was completely alone. She looked over at the boom box and took a deep breath. It had been a long time, but she couldn't resist. She turned down the volume so no one would hear what she was up to. She pressed play.

Lagoona started to dance to the music.

Her arms flowed in rhythm to the beat, her feet barely seemed to touch the floor, and her long blond curls wafted around her face like seaweed in the currents. It was as if she were moving through water not air. She seemed to defy gravity. She was surprisingly graceful. She could move!

Unknown to Lagoona, Gil had slipped into the back of the auditorium and was watching her. He couldn't believe what he was seeing. He'd never seen Lagoona dance before. As the music soared, Lagoona twirled, turning faster and faster until she was an aqua blur of movement. Without even thinking about what he was doing, Gil began to clap. Lagoona stopped in mid-turn. Her eyes were so wide they almost bulged.

Her mouth was pursed with surprise. She looked ridiculous. She looked like a frozen fish. Slowly, she began to tilt. She was going to fall right over!

Gil dove into action and ran toward the stage. He caught her just in time. "Lagoona! Are you okay?"

Lagoona blinked and looked around. What had happened? She could barely remember—and then she did. She felt so ashamed. "How long were you watching me?"

"Long enough to see you're a fintastic dancer! Who knew?"

"Nobody!" Lagoona shuddered. "And I want to keep it that way. That was just a dance we used to do Down Unda. But that's ancient history. I don't dance anymore."

She pulled herself together and turned off the music. She wanted to get away from the Vampitheater as fast as possible. She headed to her locker, Gil following her. "But why?" he persisted. "You're great, Lagoona! You should dance in the show tomorrow."

"I can't." Lagoona looked around to make sure no one was listening. Ghouls were strolling by, waving. She leaned in close to Gil, whispering. "You saw what happens. I freeze. Any time I dance in front of an audience I go belly up. I make a face like a stuck puffer fish. Luckily, you are the last monster who will ever see that again."

Robecca Steam whizzed past on her Rollerblades, almost bumping into the aquatic couple. She spun around and swerved to avoid HooDude VooDoo.

"Hey, Lagoona," HooDude called out. "Don't forget to add me to the Eek-vite for tomorrow's after-party. It's going to be voltageous."

"You got it, HooDude!" said Lagoona. She waited until he had disappeared down the hall. "You won't tell anyone about my stage fright, right, Gil?"

"Of course not," he reassured her. "Your secret is safe with me, Lagoona."

She wrapped her arms around him and gave him a great big hug. Phew! That's what Lagoona loved about Gil. He made her feel so happy, and after all they'd been through together, she knew that he really cared about her.

But her secret wasn't safe from Toralei.

The werecat had been standing, just out of eyesight, on the stair landing. She had heard everything. Everything. Her green eyes flashed wickedly. "So perfect little Lagoona freezes up like a fish stick onstage, huh? Be a shame if somebody let *that* cat out of the bag!"

She slunk off into the shadows, determined to play a terrible trick on her aquatic friend.

Chapter 3

LIKE A FISH OUT OF WATER

It was the night of the big dance recital and the clawditorium was packed with monsters, their parents, their teachers, and their friends. Everyone had come to watch the ghouls dance—and no one could believe what they were seeing. It was a truly terrible performance—maybe even worse than the rehearsal the day before. No one in the audience knew what to do. They studied their programs. They tried to smile and look supportive. They pretended they were somewhere else. But nobody wanted to watch. This was Toralei's feline fiasco.

Backstage, Lagoona was holding a box brimming with decorations and paper plates for the after-party.

She put the box down to peek through the curtains and watch what was happening onstage. Gil came up behind her, a bunch of balloons in his hands.

"You should be out there," said Gil sweetly.

Lagoona was happy swaying to the music as she watched her friends. She was dancing along with them, only they didn't know it. No one knew it.

Onstage, the ghouls had circled around Toralei as she broke out into her big solo. She might have been trying to break-dance or hip-hop or tap dance or… something. It was hard to tell what she was doing. The ghouls were clapping to the beat. Toralei careened around in a circle and threw up her arms. "Ta-da!" she announced, expecting a standing ovation.

A few people in the audience did clap. At least it was over.

"I thought cats were always supposed to land on their feet," someone heckled.

Toralei's eyes narrowed and she peered into the audience. For the first time she realized how badly the performance had gone. She was furious. She hissed and growled and stomped offstage.

"The show's not over," spat Toralei. The best way to not be embarrassed, she decided, was to embarrass someone else. She noticed Lagoona dancing by herself, completely unseen, just behind the curtain. All at once Toralei had a plan to save her reputation.

Toralei began pulling on the ropes that controlled the backstage curtains. Lagoona, listening to the music and lost in her reverie, was dancing like no one was watching. Because she didn't know that anyone was.

But the curtain was up and the whole audience could see her.

"Cool!"

"Clawesome!"

"Amazing!"

"Now that's dancing!" shouted someone.

Too late, Lagoona realized that everyone was looking at her. She rushed to hide, but her foot caught on one of the many coiled ropes backstage. A sandbag slipped and Lagoona, hanging by her ankle upside down, was pulled up, up, up into the air, swinging across the stage. She dangled upside down right in the spotlight. Her eyes widened. Her lips pursed. She was

going full fish face, just like a haddock reeled in from the sea.

"Look! Look!" exclaimed Toralei. "Frozen fish stick!"

The audience was shocked, whispering and murmuring. Except for Meowlody and Purrsephone. They pulled out their iCoffins and began snapping photos. This was too good! Everyone had to know about this.

And it wouldn't be long before everyone did.

Chapter 4

SOMETHING'S FISHY

The next day, Lagoona and Gil walked into the Creepateria. All at once monsters began whispering and pointing. They stared at Lagoona and then pretended they weren't. Everyone was checking their iCoffins—including Clawdeen, Frankie, and Draculaura. When the ghouls saw Lagoona coming over to sit down at their table, they hurried to put their phones away.

"Hey ghouls, what's up?" asked Lagoona cheerfully.

"Absolutely nothing is up," answered Draculaura, a fake smile stuck to her face.

"Definitely not watching the video of you from last night online," Draculaura said as innocently as she could.

Clawdeen and Frankie glared at her. Lagoona realized at once that something was up. She grabbed Draculaura's iCoffin. She almost couldn't believe what she was seeing.

Frozen on the screen was a still from a video of Lagoona hanging from the stage ropes. GOING BELLY UP! was the headline. Even worse? Underneath it was listed the number of people who had already watched the entire embarrassing video: 6,000,000,012 views.

Lagoona gulped. "Six…billion…views?"

Draculaura took back her phone and shut it off. "I'm sure that it's mostly one or two monsters watching it three billion times each....I'm going to shut my fangs now."

"It gets worse." Clawdeen decided it was time to break the news to their friend. As bad as it was.

"You're a Monsternet meme," Frankie explained. She handed Lagoona her iCoffin. Photo after photo showed Lagoona hanging upside down like a guppy out of water. Some had funny sayings added to the photo like HANG IN THERE! Others had been manipulated to show Lagoona hanging from monuments like the Vampire State Building.

"This is a nightmare! I'm sunk!" Lagoona was overwhelmed and ashamed.

Without thinking about what she was doing, Lagoona snatched every one of her friends' phones out of their hands. She stormed around the Creepateria confiscating iCoffins. She marched down the hallway grabbing them away from monsters. She would get rid of every phone in the entire school. She had to!

"Hey! That's my phone!"

"What the..."

Her arms filled with phones, she took a hard left toward the pool. It was decorated for the after-party with streamers and decorations and tables of food. Lagoona knew exactly how to take care of this. Every one of these phones was going in the water! And every

computer at the school and at everyone's home…
Slowly, it dawned on her how impossible it was
going to be to control this. Even her own iCoffin was
buzzing. She dropped all the phones in her arms to
answer it. It was a monster-gram with another photo.
This one showed her hanging upside down from the
Monster of Liberty.

"Crikey!"

What was she going to do? There was no way to
find six billion phones. How could she stop this? More
important, how could she get revenge? "This is all
Toralei's fault. And after all the work I did to make the
wrap party fantastic. How would she like it if she felt
like the fish out of water?"

Lagoona clicked off the image on her phone and
brought up another page. It was her Eek-vite to the
after-party. Photos of everyone who had been invited,
which was everyone at Monster High, appeared on the
screen.

Lagoona stared at Toralei's face. "Maybe it's time
she got a taste of her own medicine."

With a quick tap, Lagoona put a big red X over the
werecat's face.

"Disinvited!" said Lagoona.

If only it made her feel better.

Chapter 5

THROWN IN THE DEEP END

School was over for the day, the moon was rising, and it was time for the after-party.

Cleo handed her backpack to one of her Anubis bodyguards. The dog-headed Egyptian followed her obediently toward the pool. Cleo's iCoffin rang and she answered it. "Deuce? Hi, Snake Eyes." That was her new nickname for her Gorgon boyfriend. He actually did have snakes all over his head but not for eyes. His eyes turned anyone who looked into them into stone—which was why he always wore dark glasses.

"That dance recital was for the bats," Cleo said to Deuce, "but the after-party is what counts. See you there!"

At her locker, Toralei was packing up her backpack, looking satisfied. Her plan had worked. No one had been talking about her disappointing dance performance! Instead everyone had been laughing at Lagoona. She was one smart kitty! She pulled out her phone to check the Eek-vite again. Where was the party? That's when she saw the great big red *X* over her face.

Toralei sniffed with irritation and tucked the phone back into her pocket. She wouldn't let this stop her. How hard could it be to find a party anyway? Nobody could disinvite her. It was her idea in the first place to even *have* a party. They were probably in the catacombs under the school. That's where she'd have the party if she were throwing it.

She walked partway down the stone stairs. The

catacombs were cold and dark, dripping with water and mold. Such a great place for a celebration. "Hello?" she called out. "Party monsters?"

From out of the darkness, a giant swarm of bats flew right into Toralei's face, completely undoing all the work she had carefully done on her hair for the party. Irritated, she fled the catacombs.

Maybe all the monsters were upstairs in the attic. Toralei climbed and climbed. But when she finally got there, no one else seemed to have arrived. The only thing in the attic was a giant mirror.

Just then, another swarm of bats swooped down from the rafters. "Aack! Ppbbth!" hissed Toralei. Cobwebs and dust scattered over her dress. After she wiped herself off, she went from classroom to classroom. Where were they? From somewhere, only she didn't know where, she could hear the dull thumping of party music.

"Maybe Lagoona stuck a paper invite in my locker," she decided.

But when she opened her locker, another swarm of bats engulfed her. She swatted at them, but they evaded her effortlessly. One tiny confused bat hovered by her face and flapped its wings against her cheeks. She hurled it away from her. "Oh come on!" she exclaimed, frustrated.

Meanwhile, unbeknownst to Toralei, the party was in full swing at the pool. Lit candles floated across the surface of the water. Holt Hyde, the flame-haired DJ, was spinning discs. Students were dancing, talking, and hanging out.

"This party is freaky fangtastic!" exclaimed Draculaura.

"I know," Frankie agreed. "Ghoulia brought her clawesome creepcakes."

In addition to being the smartest student at Monster High, Ghoulia Yelps was also an amazing chef. Her creepcake creations—decorated with sprinkles, logos, and even fizzing sparklers—were impossibly impressive.

Cleo was having a very good time. "Killer party!" she yelled to Abbey over the music.

"Even with the music of loudness and the people of crowding?"

"That's what makes a killer party, Abbey," Cleo explained to the yeti.

Toralei burst through the doors to the pool. Her dress was dusty. Her hair was a mess. She was scowling. Manny Taur, standing at the door like a bouncer at a club, stopped her before she could enter the party. Spectra was looking over the names on her guest list.

Toralei tried to push past Manny. "Step aside, bull boy."

"Sorry, Toralei," he said. "We don't see your name on the Eek-vite list."

Toralei's eyes narrowed with fury.

Seeing her, Cleo giggled. Toralei was totally bedraggled. What a crazy look for a party! "Look what the cat dragged in! Herself!" Cleo joked. "See? I can be funny."

But Toralei didn't think it was funny. At all. She pushed past the ghouls in search of Lagoona. "Lagoona!" she shouted. "Prepare to be filleted!"

Clawdeen shook her head. "There's a fine line between fashionably late and just late, ghoul."

"We're glad you decided to show," said Frankie.

Toralei was about to explode with rage. "Decided? I wasn't even *invited*!"

Draculaura looked confused. "Lagoona wouldn't do that, right?"

"Oh, I invited Toralei all right," said Lagoona, joining the ghouls. "Then I uninvited her."

Toralei's claws were coming out. "How dare you uninvite me to my OWN party!"

"How dare you embarrass me in front of the entire Monsternet?" answered Lagoona. She was just as angry.

Everyone at the party stopped speaking and dancing at the same moment. They were watching the ghouls fight. All except for Ghoulia. She was the only monster who noticed that the pool had begun to glow ever so faintly. Tiny sparkly bubbles were popping on the surface of the water.

"It's on!" spat Toralei.

"Bring it!" Lagoona fumed. She wasn't going to back down. No way.

"It was just a joke," said Toralei.

"Jokes are funny." Lagoona was going to accept nothing less than a full apology.

"I laughed," snarled Toralei.

"Exactly my point! It's always about you!"

Ghoulia peered over the edge of the pool. The bubbles were bigger.

"Hey," hissed Toralei to Lagoona. "It's not my fault you went *belly up* onstage."

"You knew I would freeze! That's why you pulled back the curtain!"

The water in the pool had begun to spin, creating a whirlpool. The pale blue water had turned to an angry red. Ghoulia groaned, trying to get someone else to notice. But everyone was watching the fight between Toralei and Lagoona.

"You should thank me for trying to help you get over your stage fright!" Toralei announced.

"Thank you? Now that *is* a joke!"

"Six billion and counting," Toralei taunted.

Lagoona exploded. "Kitty litter!"

"Fish eyes!"

"Fang face!"

"Chum bucket!"

They were hurling insults back and forth. Frankie couldn't stand it. She jumped in between them. "Ghouls! It's a party! Everyone just STOP!" She took a breath and smiled. "Have a creepcake."

"Sure," said Lagoona through gritted teeth. "I'll have a couple." She grabbed handfuls of Ghoulia's creepcakes. "Maybe I'll just hog as many as I want, because I only think about *myself*."

Toralei began grabbing creepcakes too. Armfuls.

Ghoulia moaned. All the work she had done on the creepcakes was ruined, a mess of smeared frosting and scattered sprinkles. Not only that, but no one was looking at the pool—and something very strange was going on.

"Maybe I'll hide them all," shouted Toralei about the creepcakes, "and not invite anybody else to come."

"Maybe I'll film you taking them and put it all over the Monsternet!"

"Maybe I'll have a huge creepcake party and conveniently forget to invite you!"

The pool had turned an angry crimson. It was sparkling with some kind of hidden magic and the water was swirling faster and faster.

"There's only one place I can think of to fit all these creepcakes," Lagoona raged.

"Oh really?" screamed Toralei. "I can think of a place…."

"In your BIG mouth!" shouted both ghouls at the exact same moment.

Toralei reached out to smash a creepcake in Lagoona's face. Shocked, Lagoona stepped aside. Their friends were horrified. How could they get the ghouls to stop fighting?

Clawd and Heath, unconcerned, were munching down on creepcakes—until Toralei grabbed one out of Clawd's hand.

"No!" he yelled in surprise.

Toralei stumbled forward accidentally and slipped on the wet surface of the pool rim. She skidded into the pool with an enormous splash. In an instant, the churning waters whipped her around and around. She was going under!

"Rowr!" screeched Toralei. The werecat was trying to keep her head above water.

"She can't swim!" Frankie shouted.

Lagoona didn't hesitate. She knew just what to do. She was the captain of the swim team after all. "Hang on!"

Lagoona dove in, barely noticing the strange color the water had become. She wrapped an arm around Toralei. She was trying to drag her back to dry land, but the whirlpool was too strong, even for her.

Realizing the danger the ghouls were in, Gil reached out a hand to Lagoona. Clawdeen, Draculaura, and Frankie tried to anchor him with a chain of monsters all holding on to one another. But the swirling vortex was just too powerful. One by one, splash by splash, each of the girls and Gil slid into the pool.

Frankie clung to Ghoulia. Snap! Her hand detached—and the entire chain of monsters was sucked into the water.

Ghoulia looked down at the hand she was holding. It was all that was left of her friends.

Frankie's hand dove away from Ghoulia into the pool on its own, waving good-bye, before it was submerged.

They were gone. All gone.

But where? Where had the water taken them?

Chapter 6

CAT FISH!

The waters swirled, around and around, deeper and deeper. Ghouls floated by. Crumbling creepcakes drifted in the current. An iCoffin, a photo of Lagoona open on its frozen screen, drifted to the depths. A poster for the dance recital disintegrated in the water. BE YOURSELF, BE U...

It was as if the pool had absorbed all the fighting between Toralei and Lagoona. It was angry and upset.

A sea horse swam past the ghouls. Coral appeared. This didn't look like the bottom of the pool. What was happening? The ghouls were definitely in over their heads.

Lights flashed. Bubbles burbled.

"Where are we?" Frankie cried. Draculaura was even more bewildered. "More like, *what* are we?" The ghouls realized that they could breathe underwater. Even stranger, they could swim. Even stranger than that, their legs had vanished! They'd been turned into…fish!

And not just any kind of fish: Clawdeen had the body of a dogfish shark, Draculaura the long squiggles of a vampire squid, and Frankie the slithery tail of an electric eel. Gil was a manta ray and Toralei was a lionfish. Lagoona's legs were gone too, and she seemed able to swim faster than she ever had before.

"Wow!"

"Look at you!"

"You look fintastic!"

"Whoa!"

"I've lost my legs before." Frankie laughed. "But this is ridiculous."

All the monsters, except for Lagoona and Gil, who were used to swimming underwater, were struggling to get used to their fins and tails. They wafted about like astronauts in space for the first time. They weren't used to being weightless. They turned over accidentally. They floated upside down uncontrollably. They got confused about which way was up and which way was down.

It was actually kind of cool. Everyone was enjoying it—except for Toralei. "I've been fishified! This is my worst nightmare. Do something, Lagoona!"

"What do you want me to do?"

Tiny sprightly ghouls with the tails of a sea

horse swirled by, giggling and chattering in some incomprehensible undersea language.

Lagoona recognized them at once—and couldn't believe it. "These are Sea Mares! I've heard of them." She called out to them. "Hello, little friends!"

The tiny Sea Mares chattered happily, crowding around Lagoona. They began tugging at the arms of the ghouls.

"I think they want us to follow them," said Draculaura.

The only problem, for the newly aquatic monsters, was trying to swim in one direction. The ghouls flapped their arms and floundered. But eventually, with a little concentration and effort, they managed to dive down behind the Sea Mares.

In front of them lay a beautiful underwater garden. Anemones pulsed, seaweed swayed, and coral gleamed.

Toralei didn't have any interest in how beautiful everything was. She was freaking out. "So much water," she gasped. "I'm getting hydrophobic. Everything is FISHY!" She was having a total panic attack. "LAGOONA! CHANGE ME BACK RIGHT MEOW!"

"*Oh, Lagoona didn't do that. I did!*"

The ghouls spun around to discover a pretty green

ocean goddess. She was wearing an elegant dress of shimmery sea kelp. She undulated in the sea garden. "*I am Posea, daughter of Poseidon, Guardian of the Sea,*" she announced in a deep, dramatic voice. "*I keep watch over all creatures of the deep, great and small! Behold…*"

But before she could say another word, a puffer fish bounced against her head. "Hey," shouted Posea, sounding a lot more like a teen ghoul. "I told you guys to behave when I'm working on my 'goddess' thing!"

The Sea Mares tittered.

"Wait," said Lagoona to Posea. "You brought us down here?"

Posea raised her arms. "*I brought YOU, Lagoona Blue! I can command the waters at my whim.*" She paused as if waiting for the waters around them to

actually do something. Nothing happened. She raised her hands again and a tiny bubble gurgled.

"Your friends?" Posea continued. "Bit of an accident. My bad. I'm still in the goddess kiddie pool."

Lagoona was confused. "How do you know me?"

Posea wafted over to a bed of sea flowers.

"What are these?" asked Frankie. "They're gorgeous."

Posea knelt beside a drooping aquamarine blossom. "Every sea creature is represented by a plant here in my seabed. It's how we sea protectors watch over sea life. Your plant equivalent is called your 'sea lifeline.' Here's Lagoona's. See?" Her voice became all great-and-terrible goddess again. "*You are in grave danger, Lagoona!*"

The ghouls gasped in horror.

Posea looked surprised. "Okay, so maybe not 'grave,' but it's definitely a little wilted."

Irritated, the ghouls began whispering to one another.

"Bear with me," begged Posea. "I'm new at this helping-sea-creatures thing. So…" The goddess-in-training cleared her throat. "*What troubles you, ghoul?*"

Toralei swam forward. "I'll tell you what troubles ME! Cats and water do not mix!"

"The only thing troubling me," Lagoona said, "is that my friends and I are being fishnapped. Change us back and send us home," she demanded.

"This is not how sea magic works," said Posea, peeved. "*Beneath a calm surface lie troubled waters. You must dive deep, Lagoona, and face your fears!*" It was as if the words had come from someone else, someone older and wiser.

Lagoona was taken aback. "Face my fear? Um, I do that…how?"

"That's for me to know and you to find out," Posea answered, sounding just like a teenager in the Creepateria at Monster High. She realized it sounded petty and not very oracular. "Or at least for you to find out. Like I said, I'm kind of new at this." She spread her webbed fingers and parted a curtain of kelp. "*Face your deepest fear and find your way home, Lagoona. The choice is yours: sink…or swim!*"

With a last goddess-like flourish of her long arms, Posea disappeared.

Toralei pawed through the seaweed in a panic. How would she ever get home now? "She's gone! So we can't get back till Lagoona fixes some freaky flaw? Which one? She has so many."

Frankie jabbed her elbow in Toralei's side to try and keep her from being so mean. But it made Toralei lose her balance and she floated off sideways. The Sea Mares whinnied with laughter.

"What do we do now?" Draculaura wondered out loud.

"Posea said we have to sink or swim," said Frankie. She noticed the Sea Mares wriggling through an archway of coral. She tried to follow them but ended up tangled in the seaweed, upside down and backward.

But Lagoona zipped through the entrance to the coral reef with effortless speed and agility. Lagoona certainly didn't seem to have any trouble swimming. Everyone else paddled and splashed after her as best they could.

Toralei clung to what looked like a log that had settled on the ocean bottom. Maybe she'd just wait here for everyone to come back. Why should a cat have to bother with swimming anyway? But the log was not really a log. It was a giant moray eel. As it opened its giant eye and blinked at Toralei, the werecat lunged forward, kicking her tail and waving her hands. "Wait for me," she shrieked.

Poor Toralei. She was definitely in hot water now.

Chapter 7

MAKING WAVES

The ghouls were learning to swim. They swished their tails and flipped their fins. They dove through an obstacle course of coral. The more they played with being fish, the easier it got. They could go up, down, and all around. Every direction was open to them. Gil was like a gymnast doing backflips and handsprings. Draculaura careened toward a trunk of coral but managed to squeeze herself through an opening at the last minute. Frankie zapped the reef, lighting up the entire seabed. Frankie bumped into Clawdeen.

"Yeowch," squealed Clawdeen.

"Sorry, I didn't see you," Frankie apologized.

"Forget freshwater!" exclaimed Gil, delighted. "Saltwater is where it's at."

"You guys are really getting the fang of this." Lagoona was happy to see her friends having so much fun.

Even Toralei was beginning to paddle around. "Check this out! Jazz hands."

Spiny points like fur standing on end shot out of Toralei's fishy fins. Alarmed, Draculaura jetted backward.

The tiny Sea Mares wafted back and forth in front of a dark labyrinth of coral. They seemed to indicate that the monsters were to swim into the depths—but they were waving good-bye.

"Hold your sea horses!" exclaimed Clawdeen. "Where do we go from here?"

The Sea Mares pointed into the dark expanse of the ocean—and a moment later flittered away into the coral.

Draculaura gulped. "Look at all that open water."

"Posea said you have to 'dive deep,' Lagoona. To 'face your fear.'"

"Oh, I heard her all right." Lagoona sighed. "I have a sinking feeling about it in my gut. May as well follow that."

And with that Lagoona began to sink—down,

down, down into the murky depths. After a moment's hesitation, all her friends followed her. Even Toralei.

The shadows of enormous whales passed overhead. A silver reflection of the moon filtered through the waves. It was almost completely black this deep in the sea. And it was cold too.

Far ahead, Lagoona saw a faint light and the dark outline of a shape she almost thought she recognized. "Why does this look so familiar?" she wondered out loud. She began swimming faster toward a distant ridge.

As they came over the rise, they saw the strangest of sights.

"Oooh, look at the lights!" gasped Frankie.

Flickers of illumination danced and curved through the inky darkness. They shimmered and shone. There were sparkles of blue and trails of rainbows. It was one of the most beautiful things any of the monsters had ever experienced.

"What are they?" wondered Draculaura.

The ghouls swam closer and closer. It was almost as if the lights were dancing with one another and creating patterns in the darkness. The ghouls swam toward the lights.

Blam!

A spotlight burst on.

Now they could really see what they were looking at. What they were seeing weren't lights—but dancers! The fishy ballerinas were wearing what must be phosphorescent outfits that left glowing trails in the water behind them. It was like they created a fireworks show just by moving through the water.

The ghouls and Gil were at the top of a stadium looking down at the stage. All kinds of extraordinary undersea creatures were performing an underwater ballet like nothing anyone had ever seen before.

Without even realizing it, the monsters had been swimming closer and closer for a better look. They were right in the center of the stadium! The audience was all around them. Fish of all kinds were cheering and waving their fins.

Onstage, three dancers twirled in unison. One of them was clearly the star. Her partner was a two-headed sea creature with one tail. Behind them, a chorus of other dancers swayed and swooped in rhythm to the haunting ocean music.

It was clearly the very end of the dance. The dancers were turning and turning, faster and faster. The performance ended with a crash of applause and all the dancers taking a deep bow.

At the center of all the dancers was the stunning purple sea monster with four arms of tentacles; a veil

42

of dark, wavy hair; and an iridescent tail. As she rose from her curtsy, her eyes met Lagoona's. She couldn't believe it! What was Lagoona doing here?

"Lagoona!" The dancer swam right off the stage toward the ghoul.

But Lagoona didn't look happy to see someone she recognized. In fact, she looked upset. Very, very upset.

How did these two ghouls know each other?

Lagoona took a deep breath. "Hello, Kala."

Kala was smiling but her smile was cold. She looked venomous and mean. She was scary. "Like the new look," she said to Lagoona. "Beats your old two-legger style."

The sea monster moved to the edge of the stage and took the microphone. "Ladies and fishermen," Kala announced. "We have a special guest tonight. Would you like to meet her?"

The crowd went wild, cheering and clapping.

Lagoona was shaking her head. She was clearly terrified.

"Lagoona? What's going on?" asked Draculaura, concerned.

"Please welcome my old fin and dancing partner...." Kala was gesturing toward Lagoona. "Lagoona!"

Lagoona was doing the backstroke. She didn't want to get onstage. But it didn't matter. The other dancers had grabbed her arms and were pulling her up. Lagoona stared at the audience. They were a sea of faces looking at her. Her vision went blurry. She was going to pass out. She was going to freeze.

This was all too familiar.

She had been here before. A long, long time ago.

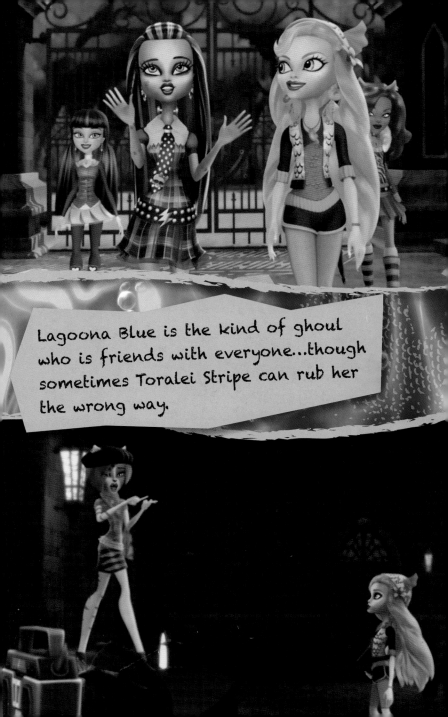

Lagoona Blue is the kind of ghoul who is friends with everyone...though sometimes Toralei Stripe can rub her the wrong way.

But that doesn't stop Lagoona
from jumping into the Monster
High pool to try to save Toralei
after she falls in.

Gil, Frankie, Draculaura,
and Clawdeen try to help.
They are all sucked into a
vortex.

They have legs when they enter the pool...and then they have tails!

They meet Posea Reef, the daughter of Poseidon.

Exploring the Great Scarrier Reef is fintastic!

Kala Mer'ri used to be Lagoona's dance partner.

Kala's friends Pearl and Peri Serpentine play a trick on Lagoona.

Why does Kala dislike Lagoona so much?

The ghouls try to avoid the Kraken!

Except for Lagoona, who wants to face her fears and look into the Kraken's eyes!

Lagoona and her ghoulfriends escape back to Monster High....

But the Kraken has followed them home!

Lagoona discovers Kala's secret. The Kraken is her dad!

Posea tends to the flowers in her garden. Lagoona's and Kala's flowers have never looked better

Chapter 8

BELLY UP

Years ago, a twelve-year-old Lagoona was rehearsing her dance moves with Kala backstage. She was graceful and every move was perfect, but Kala was clearly nervous and tripping over her tail. Gently, Lagoona helped up her friend and showed her the steps again.

"I know it's four times as hard with tentacles," Lagoona said, trying to be kind. "But at least you dance better than the Kraken!" She giggled at her own joke. The Kraken was the fearsome octopus-like monster that was supposed to live at the bottom of the ocean. It was big and ugly and it probably couldn't dance at all.

But Lagoona's words did not comfort Kala. If anything, she looked more frustrated and angry.

Onstage, the emcee was announcing the next act. "We'll be back in a few moments with Lagoona Blue and Kala Mer'ri!"

The audience was packed with people. Little Lagoona looked out at the sea of faces, but she wasn't scared; she was excited. She was brimming with confidence and so different from the teenage ghoul terrified to perform.

"It's a full house!" Lagoona exclaimed. She spotted her mother and her father and her brothers and sisters. Even her grandparents were there for the big night. "Look, Kala," she squealed, pointing from behind the curtain. "My entire family came."

Not only that but they were wearing T-shirts with Lagoona's face on them! They were her very own fan club. When they noticed her looking at them from behind the curtain, they began cheering and taking photos.

"Yay! There she is!"

"Break a fin!"

"That's our ghoul!"

Lagoona waved back happily.

Kala was pouting, but Lagoona didn't seem to notice. "My dad took off work special just to be here," she gushed. "We're having a big party afterward."

"Can I come?" Kala asked eagerly.

Lagoona seemed surprised. "Aren't you going to be with *your* family? Where are they sitting?"

Kala took a deep breath. It was almost as if she was trying not to cry. She waved her hand in the direction of the audience, landing on nobody in particular. "Over there somewhere," she said vaguely.

"Where?" asked Lagoona, peering.

"There," she answered. But she didn't point anywhere.

Lagoona in her excitement about the performance didn't notice how upset her partner was. She babbled on and on. "My dad loves to watch me dance. Maybe your dad could meet my dad. Maybe your dad and my dad will become friends like us. Maybe my dad and your dad could take us on a picnic. Maybe they're sitting on the other side? Hey, I bet your dad would really like my dad—"

"They're not coming, okay?" Kala interrupted her abruptly. Her lower lip quivered. "Only a baby would need her daddy here anyway."

"Kala!" exclaimed Lagoona, hurt. "Why are you being so mean?"

"Why do you have to be Little Miss Perfect?" Kala shot back. "With your perfect dance moves, your perfect looks, and your perfect family. You don't know what it's like to be made fun of for where you come from."

"I don't understand…." Lagoona really didn't. What was Kala talking about? But there was no more time to talk. The emcee was announcing them!

"Scalies and gentlefins, please welcome our next dance performance! The Great Scarrier Reef's very own Lagoona Blue and Kala Mer'ri!"

While Lagoona was waving one last time at her father, Kala leaned down as if she were picking up something that she'd dropped. Very quickly and quietly, Kala tied Lagoona's shoes together. It was a wicked thing to do. Not only couldn't Lagoona dance, she couldn't even walk! She tripped the moment she went to move. Instead of taking the stage with a flourish, she ended up floating sideways, pumping her arms to try and get upright again.

The audience burst into peals of laughter. They thought it was a comedy act!

"Quit clowning around, Lagoona!" whispered Kala. "You're embarrassing us!"

"Ha!"

"Lookit that two-legger!"

"Suckerfish!"

"She's tanking!"

Lagoona looked out at the hooting crowd. Worst of all, she saw her parents and her grandparents and her brothers and sisters. They looked surprised and disappointed. She had failed them all. She was totally ashamed.

It was the worst day of Lagoona's entire life—and it was the last day that she ever danced in public.

Chapter 9

HOME FROM SCHOOL

Back at the amphitheater with her Monster High friends, Lagoona tried to let go of these old, terrible memories. She tried to unfreeze. Slowly, she pulled her face into an awkward smile. But it was too late. She couldn't move her tail or her arms and she was already floating belly up.

The ghouls gasped. What was going on? What was the matter with Lagoona?

Kala's friends were surprised too. Peri and Pearl Serpentine, the hydra with two heads sharing a single serpentine tale, whispered to each other.

"Poor Lagoona, do you think she's okay, Peri?" asked Pearl.

"Pearl, she's frozen!" Peri answered.

"Just like old times," said Kala gleefully.

The crowd was erupting with laughter—just like it had when Lagoona was a twelve-year-old girl, accidentally making a fool of herself.

The ghouls rushed toward the stage to help their friend. But it was too late. Lagoona was tilting, tilting, tilting. She toppled over. As quickly as they could, the ghouls got her out of the amphitheater and away from Kala.

"Who was that poison puffer fish?" asked Clawdeen.

Toralei's spines were sticking out. Slowly, she drew them back in.

Lagoona sighed. "That's Kala and her ghoulfriends, Pearl and Peri."

"Someone like that has ghoulfriends?" Draculaura asked.

"I'm glad I'm not one of them!" exclaimed Clawdeen.

Frankie was thoughtful. "So what was Kala doing? Some sort of dance?"

"It's a classic aquatic dance we do down under," explained Lagoona. "I used to love performing it…with her. Kala is a big part of why I left the Great Scarrier Reef and came to Monster High for a fresh start."

"What happened?" Clawdeen asked.

"It's ancient history." Clearly Lagoona did not want to talk about it. "What matters now is getting everything back to normal. Tomorrow we'll find Posea and make her send us back."

"Finally! Some monster makes sense!" Toralei did not think she could stand this much longer. A school of fish swarmed past her. "Meow! Watch it! I'm swimming here."

Ahead of the ghouls was a beautiful undersea town. It was made entirely out of brilliant orange and pink corals and iridescent shells and pearls. It gleamed and glowed! Sea creatures bustled about their business.

They swam along streets that went up and down, this way and that way, in all possible directions. There were fancy stores and hip coffee shops.

"So," said Lagoona, "what do you think of my hometown?"

The ghouls were blown away. The Great Scarrier Reef was breathtaking. It was a spectacular underwater culture.

A big bass swam past the ghouls. He was walking a lobster on a leash like a dog. He pulled out a plastic bag to scoop the poop of his pet crustacean. A school of fish kids darted past with their book bags and notebooks. Lagoona led her friends through the town to a neighborhood.

"While we're down here, we can stay with my family. They'll be so surprised to see me," Lagoona said.

With a waggle of her tail, she plunged downward toward a pretty coral house perched on the edge of a steep drop into deep water. Gil hesitated. Maybe it was the ocean abyss making him feel nervous—or maybe it was meeting Lagoona's parents!

"C'mon, Gil," called Lagoona encouragingly. "Ready to meet my whole family?"

Gil swallowed hard. "Um…yay?"

Lagoona grabbed Gil's hand playfully and pulled him along into the house.

Only Toralei was still outside. She peered into the deep, deep water beside the house. It looked like the blackness never ended. How deep could it be? She gasped. It was almost as if the darkness were alive, as if *something* were moving down there. She shuddered and raced to catch up with the others. The ocean was no place for a cat!

Inside the house, Lagoona's family couldn't believe it! She was home—and summer vacation was still weeks away.

"What are you doing here?" squealed Kelpie, her little sister.

"Welcome home!" Her father, Mr. Wade Blue, was thrilled.

"Meet my dad, Wade Blue," Lagoona introduced him.

"Nice to meet you, Mr. Blue," said the ghouls politely.

Mr. Blue scratched his scales. Something had changed about his daughter, but what? "Lagoona, let me guess, new haircut?"

Lagoona giggled. Her dad could be so clueless sometimes. "Uh, I have a TAIL!"

"You crazy kids these days and your fads. I don't know how you do it."

The ghouls tried not to laugh. He was just like their fathers.

"Well, come on in," said Mr. Blue. "Let me make you some Vegebite sandwiches."

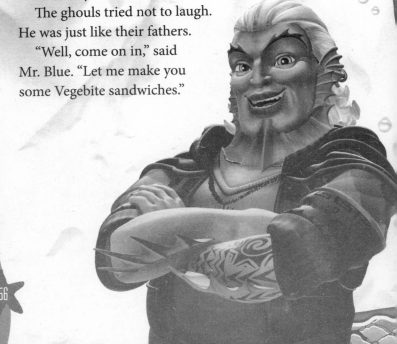

56

Chapter 10

FISHING FOR CLUES

A few houses away, Kala was sitting on a rooftop with Peri and Pearl, looking through binoculars. She had been spying on Lagoona, watching every moment of her arrival home. She pursed her lips and bulged her eyes and froze the silly expression on her face. She was mimicking Lagoona.

Pearl forced a laugh.

"She looked like that, right?" said Kala.

"Totally!" agreed Pearl. "That was SO Lagoona. You could be an actress too, Kala. You have *soooo* many talents."

Peri glared at her sister disapprovingly. Sometimes she could be such a suck-up. "Give it a rest, sis," she whispered to her other head. "Kala knows you worship the ground she floats on."

"You're just jealous," hissed her sister, "because I'm Kala's BFF. Best. Fish. Forever!"

"Pearl, you have such a big head sometimes," Peri snapped.

"At least mine's not an *air*head!" answered Pearl, slapping at her sister's hand.

"Watch it! My manicure!" cried Peri.

"Don't be so shallow!"

Kala couldn't have been more bored. "Will you two put a hook in it and stop bickering? I'm trying to spy."

Kala picked up her binoculars again. She focused them on a window in Lagoona's house. She was trying to see what was going on. What was Lagoona up to? Why was she back? That was the question.

All the ghouls were hanging out in the family room while Lagoona's younger brothers and sisters bobbed around them excitedly. Dewey, holding a stuffed clown fish, wriggled close to Toralei. She was filing her nails and she was not amused. Her spikes flared and she glared at him. Dewey swam backward as fast as he could.

Lagoona's dad was catching her up on the family news. "Lagoona, your mom is going to be sad she missed you all, but she's visiting your aunt Bay all weekend."

"That's too bad," said Lagoona, disappointed.

"Help!" yelped Gil. All of Lagoona's brothers and her sister were climbing over him like he was a jungle gym. They squiggled and wiggled and tickled.

"Dewey! Squirt! Tadpole!" Lagoona called. "Not so rough!"

Gil reached through a scrum of kids to wave. "I'm okay," he said, his voice muffled.

The ghouls burst out laughing—except for Lagoona. She was distracted. Being home brought back so many memories and stirred up so many feelings. She stared through the window at the deep, dark ocean trench.

Kelpie swam over to her big sister. "I missed you, Lagoona."

"I missed you too, Kelpie!" Lagoona hugged the little girl, truly happy to see her, but she sighed heavily at the same time. There was a lot on her mind.

Clawdeen noticed that something was wrong with Lagoona, but she didn't say anything. Still, she wondered. Why had Posea brought Lagoona home and what fear was she really supposed to confront?

Chapter 11

TAKING THE PLUNGE

The morning sunlight filtered through the water. The entire Scarrier Reef brightened and sparkled! A sea rooster paddled over to a white picket fence outside Lagoona's house and began gurgling and crowing to ring in the new day.

Clawdeen yawned and stretched. Something felt funny. That's right! Her legs were gone and she still had a fish's tail.

In the kitchen, Lagoona's dad was reading the newspaper. A giant blurry photo of a huge monster with a bulging head and giant tentacles covered the front page.

"Tsk tsk." Mr. Blue sighed. "Another Kraken sighting."

"What's a Kraken?" asked Toralei, coming in from the other room. She had been teaching some of her awful dance moves to Lagoona's little sister.

"You don't know what a Kraken is?" Mr. Blue was genuinely surprised. "It's a horrific beast that swims up at night to terrorize schools of fish."

Draculaura gulped. "Is it dangerous?"

"*Dangerous* doesn't even begin to cover it, little lady. He lives in the deepest, darkest part of the ocean, over at the edge of town. They say nobody who has looked the horrible, stinking Kraken in the eye has lived to tell the tale!"

The ghouls all looked nervous. Hopefully they would be heading back to Monster High very soon. Hopefully before night fell again.

"Dad, stop scaring my friends," scolded Lagoona. "We need to find Posea, get our legs back, and get her to send us back to Monster High."

"But Posea said we can't get back until you face your fear," Frankie noted.

"What *fear*?" snapped Lagoona. "What am I meant to be afraid of?"

The ghouls exchanged glances. Wordlessly, they all imitated Lagoona going belly up onstage. They weren't making fun of her; they were just trying to help her out.

Lagoona dropped her head into her hands, ashamed. "So I have terrible stage fright."

But then she realized something and brightened. "Hey! What if I've already done it? Faced my fear? I *was* just onstage again. Briefly. Last night. And I survived."

Draculaura didn't look so sure, remembering Lagoona toppling over. "I don't know…"

"Nope, I'm sure I'm done," Lagoona announced. She seemed a little unhinged. "We just need to find Posea and tell her!"

Kelpie burst into the room before the ghouls could contradict Lagoona. "Can I hang out with you today?"

"Not today, Kelpie. The ghouls and I have something important to do."

"But you're not *leaving* leaving, right?"

Lagoona smiled at her little sister. "We'll talk about it later."

Kelpie smiled hopefully and swam off to wrestle Gil again. All the serpent kids were suctioning themselves to him.

"Let's play barnacles!" Dewey exclaimed to Gil.

"Gil?" Lagoona called.

"Coming!" he answered, trying to peel off the kids who were attached to him.

Lagoona led her friends out of the house toward the

finny golf course at the end of the street. It was right next to the giant abyss.

"Swimmy golf!" said Frankie, reading the entrance sign. "That looks fun!"

"No time for games, ghouls!" Lagoona answered. "We need to find Posea today."

Frankie, Draculaura, and Clawdeen swam past the finny golf course with its water wheels and windmills. Reluctantly, they peered over the edge into the trench.

"This does look like where the scariest, meanest beast ever would live," remarked Clawdeen.

"Let's just hope it stays HOME!" Draculaura wished.

"Creepy," agreed Toralei. "I mean, who's to say it won't just POP UP right…*meow*!"

The ghouls screamed.

Something was coming out of the darkness!

But it was only the Sea Mares. They were giggling. Streams of little bubbles floated up around them. But a moment later Posea herself emerged from behind the finny golf sign.

"You ghouls have really found your sea legs. Or sea tails. Ha! Even the Kraken would be impressed, and he's mostly sea legs. Or tentacles, technically." Posea was in a more conversational, less goddess-like mood.

"Okay, Posea, I did it," said Lagoona, confronting

her. "I faced my fear. Just like you asked. Done-zo."

Posea wrinkled her forehead. "Really? That was fast. Too fast. Suspiciously fast."

"Not too fast," Lagoona argued. "Exactly the right speed. Home and legs now, please."

"Ah-ah!" answered Posea, thinking. "Let's just check your sea lifeline."

With a wave of her arms, Posea materialized a large screen transmitting a watery picture of her garden. She zoomed in on Lagoona's flower. It was still wilted. In fact, it even seemed a little droopier.

"Hmmm," considered Posea. "Sorry."

"But I'm sure that I faced it! I know I did!"

Clawdeen shook her head. "Not according to Wilty McFlower here."

"Clawdeen!" Lagoona turned on her friend, angry. "NOT helping. Please, Posea. It's not fair."

"I told you," said the sea goddess, *that's not how sea magic works. Face your deepest fear and find your way home—*"

Lagoona interrupted her. "How am I supposed to know when I've faced it? I don't know sea magic!"

Posea drew herself up until she looked strangely commanding. "Lagoona Blue! Have patience! Go with the flow and let the answers wash over you like a wave."

And with these final commands, Posea disappeared into a passing school of fish.

The Sea Mares swam away as well, tittering.

Lagoona looked very upset. Hoping to make her feel better, Draculaura suggested a round of swimmy golf.

It was just what the ghouls needed. Frankie teed off, hitting her ball right through the holes in a sunken ship. The ball landed in the lap of a skeleton pirate. A hole in one!

Lagoona tried to focus on the game, but she couldn't stop thinking about what Posea had said. "The answers will wash over me? Go with the flow? What's all that supposed to mean? What a bunch of seaweed."

"Maybe it means you should take a bath," joked Frankie. "Get it? Bath. Wash over you?"

Seeing the look on Lagoona's face, Draculaura jumped in. "Maybe it means you'll know it when you see it."

Unseen by the ghouls, Kala drifted down from above. Peri and Pearl were with her. Kala knocked away the pirate skeleton and draped herself across the throne.

"I thought you would have slunk back to Monster High by now," she said to the ghouls.

"Don't take the bait, Lagoona," warned Toralei. "Kala's just trolling you."

"Ah, Lagoona," Kala sneered. "Catfish got your tongue?"

"That's not very nice, Kala," said Peri, alarmed.

Pearl lashed out at her. "Kala will decide when it's very nice. Or she'll decide when she's just nice enough."

Lagoona interrupted their squabbling. "What do you want?" she asked Kala.

"I wanted to see if you ghouls have the guts to compete in the Siren of the Sea talent show tomorrow night."

"The best aqua dancers will be there," gushed Peri.

For the first time since coming under the ocean, Toralei looked excited. So did the other ghouls. This must really be fun. A talent show! More important, it might be the way for Lagoona to confront her stage fright—for real.

"This is what Posea meant!" Draculaura exclaimed.

Kala raised an arched eyebrow. "I hear there's an opening in the comedy category, Lagoona."

"I'm not taking the bait, Kala," answered Lagoona. "You'll have to laugh at something else."

Kelpie, Lagoona's little sister, chose that moment to reveal she'd been hiding behind a pirate treasure chest. "You just gotta! Do it, Lagoona!" It didn't help matters that she turned out to be a big fan of Kala's. "Oh my guppy, Kala! I'm, like, your biggest fan!"

Lagoona scolded her. "Kelpie, you sneaky little eel. You're not supposed to be here." She took her sister by the hand, but Kelpie pulled away.

"Please don't send me home," she begged. "I'm learning to dance, just like you!"

She began showing off her dance moves.

Kala smiled wickedly. "Aren't you the cutest little minnow? One day you are going to grow up and be just like *me*."

"Really?" asked Kelpie, enchanted by Kala.

"If you're lucky. Gee, I bet you'd sure like to see your big sister aqua dance in the Siren of the Sea competition. I'm doing it."

"'Goona!" Kelpie begged. "Oh please, you just gotta! I want to see you dance! Pretty please with oyster sauce on top?"

Lagoona crossed her arms stubbornly. She didn't want to do this. "Kelpie, it's really complicated."

"Is it?" asked Kala. "Or are you just afraid to take me on?"

The ghouls looked at Lagoona. This was it, wasn't it? They waited expectantly for her to say something.

She was really struggling. She just wanted to go back to Monster High. She did not want to ever get back onstage again. Ever. But what could she do? "I'll do it," she agreed at last. "I'll dance."

Far beneath them, the sea floor trembled as if with a distant earthquake.

"Fintastic!" exclaimed Kala gleefully. "I can't wait to see what you come up with. Or should I say...*belly up* with?"

Kala and Pearl laughed maliciously, but Peri looked embarrassed.

When Kala and the two-headed sea monster had swum away, Gil tried to reassure Lagoona. "Don't worry," he told her.

"Lagoona, are you okay?" asked Frankie. "You're looking a little shaky."

"I think I'm going to be seasick," Lagoona whispered.

"Wait, me too!" Clawdeen agreed.

But it wasn't just about the upcoming performance. The golf course was shaking. The whole ocean was shaking.

"What is that? Earthquake?" wondered Draculaura.

"That's no earthquake," gasped Lagoona. "That's the...KRAKEN! Quick, swim for it!"

Lagoona snatched up Kelpie and all the ghouls paddled as fast as they could back to town.

Out of the trench emerged a giant, squiggling tentacle. It was covered in big, sticky suckers. It groped around the golf course until it touched the throne Kala had been sitting on. The tentacle wrapped itself around it and, with a quick twitch, pulled it back into the abyss and disappeared.

But how long would it stay gone?

Chapter 12

SWIMMING AGAINST THE TIDE

The ghouls practiced their dance moves back at the amphitheater. Without legs, they felt more awkward than ever. Toralei was trying to choreograph some new steps, but they were terrible. Lagoona was trying to get up her nerve to join in, but she couldn't.

Kelpie tried to encourage her sister. "So what kinda dance are you going to do, Lagoona?"

"I don't know. Got any ideas, li'l fish?"

She did!

Kelpie began leaping and twirling with joyful abandon. Her enthusiasm was infectious and Lagoona managed to join her playful sister. For a moment she danced with unself-conscious grace.

"How about like this," suggested Kelpie. "And then this, and then a whoosh!"

"I'll do my best." Lagoona laughed breathlessly.

Toralei held out her hand to Lagoona. "C'mon, learn from the master."

Lagoona hesitated. Awkwardly, she took Toralei's extended paw. "Okay."

"Trust me," said Toralei confidently. "Now. Fright, six, seven, eight."

The ghouls danced. Sort of.

Clawdeen accidentally camouflaged herself and Draculaura bumped into her, squirting a jet of black ink across the stage. Toralei's spikes came out accidentally and poked Frankie. Alarmed, Frankie zapped everyone with electricity. The ghouls' dancing was worse than ever.

Watching from the bleachers, Kala was delighted. "They're terrible! I love it!"

Peri was concerned. "Maybe we should help them do better."

"Why?" asked Pearl. "They're flopping perfectly on their own."

"Put a flipper in it," Kala snapped. "I'm watching."

Peri leaned close to her other head. "Pearl, this is mean. Kala is a bully. You've got to get your head out of the clouds and back in the water. She's not our real friend."

"Are you saying Kala is two-faced?" Pearl whispered back. "Trust me, I would know!"

Peri sighed. "If we can't put our heads together, we'll have to agree to disagree."

"That's the smartest idea to come out of your mouth all day!" Pearl turned away from her sister, her hand on their hip.

"Will you two clam up?" Kala asked angrily. She didn't want anything to get in the way of her enjoyment. Lagoona and her ghoulfriends were

terrible. This dance performance would be the worst ever.

Onstage the ghouls were defeated and exhausted— and they'd all just been blasted with another jolt of accidental electricity from Frankie.

With weary optimism, Toralei tried to encourage them. "Okay, we may need a little more practice."

Kelpie was clapping. "I thought you did amazing! Well, I mean, parts of it were definitely okay."

Lagoona smiled at her sister. "I'm glad, Kelpie."

"Maybe we should take five," Clawdeen suggested.

"Yeah." Lagoona laughed. "Five hundred years."

Frankie had an idea. She grabbed her iCoffin. "Why don't I record this run-through?"

"Great idea!" enthused Draculaura. "We can see where we need work."

"NO! NO PHONES! NO RECORDING!" Lagoona shouted, alarmed. She was practically in a state of shock.

"Oh!" Frankie realized her mistake at once. After what had happened with the video of her going viral, of course Lagoona was frightened of it happening again. "I'm so sorry. I didn't even think."

"Frankie would never embarrass you," Draculaura said, trying to reassure Lagoona. "She's your friend."

"We're all your friends," said Toralei.

The ghouls stared at Toralei in disbelief. After all, she was the one who had posted the video in the first place.

Toralei swallowed, embarrassed. "Sometimes."

The memory of that terrible experience had erased what little confidence Lagoona had mustered. "I'm so sorry. I just don't know if I can…." she muttered as she swam away.

Her friends watched her go, worried. How could they help her?

Chapter 13

HOOK, LINE, AND SINKER

Much later that night, everyone was fast asleep at Lagoona's. All of Lagoona's siblings had dragged their pillows and blankets around Gil's bed to stay close to him.

Gil was talking in his sleep. "No, no jumping on Gil right now."

Lagoona was gently swaying back and forth in a hammock. But she wasn't asleep. She stared at the ceiling, wondering what she was going to do. If only she could go back to Monster High. Why did she have to perform? Why did she have to get over her stage fright anyway?

Someone was tapping at the window. Lagoona

looked up. She saw Peri with a finger held to her mouth, trying to be as quiet as possible. Her sister, Pearl, was asleep, with her head resting on her shoulder. Very carefully, Lagoona opened the porthole-shaped window.

Peri looked very nervous. "My sister and Kala would flip if they knew I were doing this, but I can't take it anymore. They're mean to you and it is wrong. I want to tell you why Kala is so fearless. Kala goes down to the Deepest Dark."

Lagoona was stunned. "The Deepest Dark?"

"Yes, and the Darkest Deep," said Peri, seeming a little unhinged. "Weekly, when everyfish is at Sunday dinner, she sneaks down. I've seen her do it. She faces the ultimate fear."

"The ultimate fear?" Lagoona whispered.

"The Kraken!" Peri began talking very fast, as if she were frightened her sister would wake up at any moment. "Legend has it that if you look the Kraken dead in the eye and survive, then nothing will ever make you afraid again."

Lagoona took a deep breath. "Posea said I must face my fear to fix my freaky flaw." She was thoughtful for a minute. "But why are you telling me this?"

"Kala swims around like she owns the place. She never lets us take center stage. Mostly I am sick of her pushing my sister around."

"Thank you, Peri. Your sister is lucky to have you," said Lagoona with great sincerity. "So to get over my stage fright, I have to look the Kraken in the eye?"

Peri glanced around nervously. "I've said too much already…." With a flip of her tail, she swam back out of the porthole. Lagoona watched her swim away while she thought about what this all meant.

When Peri reached the street, Kala was waiting for her.

Kala was giggling. "Did she fall for it?"

Pearl opened her eyes. "Hook. Line. And sinker."

"You were pretending to be asleep?" Peri was confused. She felt betrayed. What had she just done? She thought she was helping—not laying a trap.

"Kala warned me that you were going softer than a sandbank," explained Pearl. "She knew you'd try something like this…."

"Poor, predictable Peri. Once Lagoona gets a look at my…at the Kraken, she'll wobble like a bowl of jellyfish."

Kala and Pearl tittered maliciously. This was going to be more fun than anything!

Lagoona's friends were worried when she told them what Peri had said. Lagoona had woken them all up to share the news.

"Okay, so to face your fear, you have to seek out the most super insanely dangerous creature in the entire

Great Scarrier Reef? No thanks," said Toralei.

Frankie was also uncertain. "Peri is pulling our legs. Or, our fins, I guess."

"Let me get this straight," Draculaura said. "You're going to face your fear by facing something way, way scarier?"

Frankie spoke her mind. "Have you gone off the deep end?"

Clawdeen laughed. "Relax, ghouls. Lagoona's kidding. Right? Lagoona? We're not going to."

"It's way too dangerous," explained Frankie.

"Scary dangerous," Draculaura agreed.

"Beyond dangerous," added Clawdeen.

Toralei nodded. "For once, I agree with Clawdeen."

Lagoona looked from one friend to another. "Then it's settled."

"Good!" the ghouls exclaimed together.

But Lagoona, unnoticed by her friends, was staring down into the dark depths with a very determined look on her face.

Chapter 14

DEEP-SEA DIVE

Gil was pretending to be a sea monster and the kids were stomping all over him. "I am the disgusting, slimy Kraken," he roared.

The ghouls were dancing with Kelpie, and Mr. Blue was serving snacks. Nobody noticed when Lagoona slipped out of the house. She looked back once at the happy scene, wishing she could stay, but she had to do what she had to do—and there was no reason to put her friends in danger.

She reached the edge of the abyss and looked down into the darkness. She took a deep breath, preparing to dive.

"And where do you think you're going?" Clawdeen demanded.

The ghouls had noticed Lagoona leaving after all. They were all there, right behind her. Not only Clawdeen but Draculaura, Frankie, and even Toralei.

Maybe it was the weight of all the ghouls on the very edge of the cliff, but the ground beneath their fins started to crumble. They jumped back just in time.

"Are you really thinking this through, Lagoona?" asked Frankie.

She nodded. "I understand if you ghouls don't want to come with me. But this is something I have to do. I'm going to face that Kraken. Ghouls, I ran away from my stage fright when I was just a tadpole. But I couldn't escape, even at Monster High. I keep trying to run from it, and it keeps finding me. It's time to rip it outta me once and for all. Even if it means staring a huge, slimy monster right in his gelatinous, disgusting eye!"

The ghouls looked doubtful. But what could they do? Lagoona was their friend—and friends stuck by one another through thick and thin, light and dark, good times and totally terrifying scary times too.

"You aren't going alone," announced Frankie, resolved.

"Yeah," Draculaura agreed.

"Right," chimed in Clawdeen.

Only Toralei was hesitant. "Are you serious?"

Lagoona was and so were the ghouls. Totally serious.

She took a step closer to the abyss. Again, it started crumbling.

"Do you hear that?" Draculaura whispered nervously to Frankie.

Out of the darkness emerged the Sea Mares. They were chittering and chattering in their incomprehensible language—but the looks on their faces said everything. What was Lagoona going to do?

"We're going to see the Kraken," she said, determined.

As if in response to her words, the Sea Mares began swimming faster and faster in a circle, creating a whirlpool of water. Posea emerged, yawning.

"Five more minutes, Dad," she whined sleepily. She blinked, noticing the ghouls. "Oh! It's you guys!"

"Can you help us get down to the Deepest Dark?" asked Lagoona.

Posea went full goddess. "*In the Deepest Dark resides the one whose tentacles can turn the tides—*"

"The Kraken. Trust me, we know," interrupted Clawdeen.

"I figured it out," Lagoona explained to Posea. "Once I face the Kraken, the scariest thing ever, I'll get over my stage fright. I'll have faced my fear!"

Posea seemed disappointed. She scrunched up her face trying to think of what to say. At last, all she could advise Lagoona was that sometimes facing your fears was harder than you imagined. "Things aren't always what they seem," she said.

Still, she lowered tendrils of kelp, like divers' ropes, deep into the trench. Little lights glowed along the kelp. Posea shook her head sadly before disappearing with the Sea Mares.

"That Posea is such a drama queen," complained Toralei.

The ghouls swam to the edge and looked down. The lights only made it seem deeper as they became smaller and smaller, fainter and fainter, disappearing at last into the darkness.

"Ready, ghouls?" Lagoona gulped.

Clawdeen wasn't so sure. "My mom always used to say, 'If all your friends jumped off a cliff, would you jump too?'"

The ghouls jumped—and Clawdeen followed an instant later. "Sorry, Mom!" she shouted as she fell through the water.

Down, down, down the ghouls fell. It seemed like a bottomless pit.

But it wasn't, and finally, after their long descent, the ghouls settled on the soft, bleak ocean floor. The tiny kelp lights far above them were useless down here.

"Ghouls, we've hit rock bottom," announced Lagoona.

"I'm scared," Draculaura whispered. "I can't see."

"It's okay," Frankie said comfortingly. "I have your hand."

Draculaura gasped. "That's not my hand!"

"I have…Clawdeen's hand?" whimpered Frankie.

"Nope!" answered Clawdeen.

Frankie was trying to quell her panic. "Toralei's?"

"Not it," said the feline.

"Then whose hand?" Frankie let loose a giant charge of electricity and the entire underwater landscape was illuminated. It was as bleak and rocky as a moonscape. But there were lots of strange bottom-feeders zooming about. A particularly creepy one—with blank eyes and needle teeth—had its fin resting in Frankie's hand.

"Aaaaaaahhhhhh!" screamed the ghouls, swimming away as fast as they could.

Ocean geysers belched up black sulfuric water. Bright red crabs scuttled through the silt. Fish that

85

created their own light streaked past them like shooting stars. Instinctively, the ghouls swam like a school of fish. They clustered together for security.

Huge boulders loomed in front of them. Some of them were as big as buildings. A path seemed to lead among them.

As they swam closer, Clawdeen noticed that something was carved on one of the giant stones. "Ghouls! There's something here," she called.

Frankie swam closer. The electric light from her eel's tail revealed the sculpture of a ghoul. Clawdeen touched it—and it was like turning it on. It glowed with a beautiful purple light.

There was another carving, and Draculaura touched it. It too popped with light, this time a rich green.

There was a whole chain of carvings, running the entire length of the boulder. Each was a different color—and yet every one of them was of a ghoul with four arms or, maybe, tentacles.

Frankie blinked. "It sort of looks like…"

"Kala," noted Lagoona. "Weird."

They followed the glowing sculptures around the boulder, deeper and deeper among the stones. At last they came to a kind of natural undersea cave. Blasts of black smoke wafted up defensively around the entrance. The tiny bleached skeletons of fish were scattered in the sand. The giant skeleton of a shark had settled right by the mouth of the cave. There was even the rusting hulk of a crushed car and the giant columns of a long-gone whale's entire rib cage.

"I thought being a fish was bad, but being fish *food* would be way worse," muttered Toralei.

"Posea said I need to face my fear." Lagoona sighed. "There's no other way…."

"It's too dangerous!" exclaimed Frankie.

"We should turn back," Clawdeen agreed.

Lagoona stared beyond the black smoke into the cave. "You ghouls are right. You should turn back. Forgive me."

With a flick of her tail, Lagoona stirred up a concealing cloud of silt.

The ghouls coughed and rubbed their eyes.

"No, wait!"

"Stop, Lagoona!"

But she was gone. "No more belly up," she told herself. She had to face her fears.

Chapter 15

BIG FISH

The ghouls watched as Lagoona wove through an obstacle course of dangers—geysers spewing acidic smoke and vacuum sand pits sucking everything down beneath the ocean floor. Lagoona darted this way and that across a terrible crevasse.

"I can't look!" Draculaura covered her eyes.

"No, Lagoona!" cried Clawdeen.

Up, down, this way, and that way. Wherever Lagoona swam, she was blocked by some horrible danger.

"You ghouls thinking what I'm thinking?" asked Frankie.

They nodded, determined. Except for Toralei.

"That we should head back up to the Great Scarrier Reef for some sushi?" she suggested. She noted the look of horror on her friends' faces. "Fine, we should help her."

"Let's get Kraken!" joked Frankie.

A little laughter, even a bad pun, helped. They linked hands to cross the minefield of dangers. Toralei used her spikes like a sail and was able to break right before a plume of sulfur hit her in the face. Draculaura elongated herself to squeeze between two geysers. With a bolt of electricity, Frankie shot over a deadly blast. Clawdeen camouflaged herself. She looked just like a rock.

But that did not make much of a difference. "Not clawesome at all," she said.

They all eventually made it to the other side using their new fish talents. They tumbled on top of one another right in front of the entrance to a giant cavern built from boulders.

"You ghouls followed me?" Lagoona couldn't believe it.

"Even if this is crazy and super dangerous, we're not letting you go alone," said Clawdeen, catching her breath. "Even if this is stupid," Clawdeen repeated.

"And super dangerous," continued Frankie. "And crazy."

"Or all of the above!" added Toralei.

"You'll never, ever go it alone," Draculaura promised.

Lagoona was really touched. But they were also right outside the Kraken's lair. There was no time for talk. Lagoona led the way into the vast cave.

Inside it was the remains of a sunken ship. Lagoona looked around. "This must be where the Kraken keeps his victims to eat them later," she said out loud.

Nobody else said a word. They couldn't. They were too scared.

The ghouls swam over to the ship, terrified about what horrors they might see. As they swam slowly below decks, looking around here and there, they were completely startled to discover a…bedroom. It was a girl's bedroom. There was a frilly comforter on the bed; pretty shell toys on the shelves; and a big, round mirror on the wall. If the Kraken lived here, he must be much, much smaller than they imagined.

In a corner of the room was the throne from the swimmy golf course. A plush squid toy was on its seat. Lagoona picked it up and squeezed it. It squeaked. Was this some trick of the Kraken's to disarm her? Was it some kind of trap?

The mirror caught Lagoona's eye. "Okay, Lagoona Blue," she told herself. "You can do this. You can look the Kraken in the eye." She bulged her eyes and pursed her lips, making her "belly up" frozen face. It would be worth it never to feel like that again.

"'Ello, Mr. Kraken!" she called out. "Are you looking at me? Are you looking at me? You must be, 'cause I don't see anyone else here."

The mirror blinked.

The ghouls froze, stunned by terrified surprise.

"That's no mirror!" realized Lagoona.

The mirror blinked again. It wasn't a mirror. It was an eye. A giant eye. The Kraken's eye. The Kraken was looking right at Lagoona!

The ground trembled. The Kraken roared!

"The Kraken!" screamed Lagoona.

One wall of the cave wasn't a wall. It was the Kraken—a gigantic squid with eight giant suction-cupped tentacles. The suckers smashed and stuck. The Kraken had a huge, sharp beak opening and shutting. It had two giant eyes. It was angry.

The ghouls swam for their lives and the Kraken took chase.

They zigged and zagged through the plumes of sulfur, but the Kraken roared right through them, spreading smoke everywhere.

"Swim, ghouls, swim," Lagoona begged her friends.

The ghouls darted up and down, trying to evade the Kraken's tentacles.

The Kraken was opening his beak to devour Draculaura. It looked like she was just about to become a Kraken cracker when she managed to squeeze into a tiny crevice in the rocks. The Kraken turned on Clawdeen, who fled into a kelp forest. She lost the Kraken by camouflaging herself and looking like a piece of seaweed. Frankie zapped the Kraken when it swam near her and Lagoona zipped superfast through the water. Each of them had special fishy ways of staying safe.

Finally, somehow, they all reached the long strands of kelp ropes Posea had let into the trench for them.

The Kraken snapped at the kelp with his beak. His tentacles slithered and probed, squished and sucked. The ghouls dangled and climbed. Would they make it?

They clambered up and up, at last reaching the edge of the cliff. The edge of the cliff crumbled, but they managed to crawl up over it in time. With a last enraged roar, the Kraken sank back into the dark.

The ghouls lay in the sand, exhausted.

"Lagoona, you did it!" Clawdeen said when she had caught her breath.

Lagoona smiled. It was true. "I did. I did it! I really did it!" She looked at each of her friends. "Thanks to you guys."

"How do you feel?" asked Frankie.

"I don't know," Lagoona admitted. "The same? Different?"

"Are you ready to take on Kala at the Siren of the Sea?"

Lagoona was beaming with pride and confidence. "There's only one way to find out."

Happily, the ghouls swam away to the amphitheater for one last practice.

Little did they know that Kala had been watching everything.

Chapter 16

SINK OR SWIM

Back at Lagoona's, Gil was working on an art project with the kids. They adored their older sister's boyfriend—and he was beginning to get used to their adoration.

"Look, I just drew a monster. He looks like Lagoona!" Dewey laughed.

"Yeah, he does," Squirt agreed.

"Your drawing stinks. Mine's better!" bragged Tadpole.

The kids started flinging paint and glitter at one another—and at Gil, who didn't seem to mind.

Mr. Blue shook his head, watching them. "C'mon, squirts. Ready to see Lagoona aqua dance?"

"Almost ready," said Gil. He stood up and spread his manta ray wings. All across his back, the kids had painted a heart-shaped framed portrait of…Lagoona!

"Ta-da!" shouted the kids, pleased with their work.

"Now we're ready." Gil laughed.

They all headed to the outdoor amphitheater. The lights on the stage glowed. There was music booming across the water. Fish creatures were streaming in from every direction.

Backstage, Lagoona was nervous. She was pacing back and forth underneath a poster advertising, APPLE AND THE TALES DEBUT PERFORMANCE COMING SOON! The rest of the ghouls were practicing their moves one last time.

"Is Lagoona's stage fright really cured?" Toralei whispered to Clawdeen.

"Do you care?" growled Clawdeen.

"Yes!" meowed Toralei. "And not just because I want to win."

Clawdeen was surprised. "You really do feel bad about what you did to Lagoona."

"I didn't say that." Toralei sniffed. But it was clear that she did. Ghouls could change, and Toralei was happy that they were getting along—and dancing together too.

"Who knew that turning you into a fish would

make you less catty?" Clawdeen laughed.

Toralei's spikes jutted out, but she smiled.

Gil slipped backstage with Mr. Blue and the kids.

Mr. Blue wrapped a fin around Lagoona. "I'm so proud of you," he told her.

"But I haven't done anything yet!"

"You're getting onstage again. You've already won in my book," her father assured Lagoona.

"Mine too," agreed Draculaura.

"Mine three!" Gil smiled.

"I wanna be brave like you, 'Goona," piped Kelpie. She hugged her sister before heading out into the audience with the rest of her family.

Kala, watching from across the room, snickered. Pearl giggled. Peri looked embarrassed.

"I'd ask why you aren't warming up, but I guess you're getting ready to FREEZE!" Kala chuckled.

"Most monsters would just say, 'Break a fin,'" said Frankie.

"How'd the field trip go?" Kala asked. "I'm sure it was *deeply* relaxing."

"Not exactly…" Clawdeen stopped in mid-sentence. "Wait a second. How'd you know about that?"

"I swear, I didn't know it was a trap! They got in my head!" exclaimed Peri.

Lagoona's face fell. She felt like she couldn't catch

her breath. "Wait," she gasped. "You tricked me?"

Kala smiled devilishly. "Were you terrified? I'm sure! As everyone likes to remind us, he's quite hideous."

"B-but I faced my fear...." stuttered Lagoona.

"So sorry." Kala sneered. "There's no magic in that Kraken's eyes. There's nothing in there but a good joke. You're still the same belly-upping fish you've always been."

Peri was appalled at how mean Kala was. Even Pearl looked uncomfortable.

"Peri! Pearl!" snapped Kala. "Stop being such sea sponges and let's go already."

Peri raised her eyebrows at Pearl, and Pearl nodded as if she understood at last. Kala was too mean. But they swam after Kala even so.

Lagoona was devastated. "It was all a joke," she cried.

"It's going to be okay," comforted Frankie.

"We have your back." Draculaura placed a reassuring hand on Lagoona's shoulder.

Frankie chimed in. "So what if there's no magic? You were brave enough to face a Kraken! What's a little dance show after *that*?"

Lagoona tried to smile—but her face looked like it was about to go full fish. "Uh-oh," she realized. She took a deep breath. It was true. She had faced the Kraken. She'd been humiliated in front of billions of people on the Monsternet. What was the worst thing that could happen? So what if she froze again?

"Ready?" asked Clawdeen.

"As I'll ever be," Lagoona answered, resolved.

From the stage, the emcee announced the next contestants. "Lagoona Blue and the Monster High dance team!"

The lights dimmed. The ghouls took their places onstage. From the audience, Lagoona's brothers and sister shouted encouragement.

The music began.

Chapter 17

DEADLIEST CATCH

In the dark, each ghoul began to move, tracing a pattern of glimmering phosphorescence through the water. One by one, the spotlight lit up each ghoul, revealing her unique moves. Frankie arched and glided. Clawdeen dazzled. Draculaura soared upward and twirled. Toralei did something kind of weird, but also a little interesting because of her spikes. Each ghoul danced away. Eventually Lagoona was left, standing alone in the middle of the stage.

The spotlight illuminated her.

She spun around, twirling up, up, up. She looked like a display of fireworks, with her gleaming trails of phosphorescence. She was a glorious blur of magical light. She was a wonder. She extended her arms and paused. She looked out at the audience for the first time. There were so many faces. They were all looking at her. She felt blurry and woozy.

"Oh no," whispered Draculaura.

Lagoona blinked and tried to clear her head. She dove downward. She reached the bottom of her plunge and spun around, but she couldn't help it. She couldn't stop thinking about all those faces staring at her. She looked out at the audience again. She stumbled.

"You can do it," whispered Frankie.

But Lagoona stopped dancing. She froze.

She was going belly up. The familiar silly look was transforming her face. She was tilting, about to topple over.

Kala was gleeful. "Look! Frozen fish stick!"

Toralei winced. That's exactly what she'd said when this had happened at Monster High. She'd been as mean as Kala to Lagoona. It upset her to realize that. A lot.

People in the audience gasped. Mr. Blue yelled out encouragement. Gil held his breath.

Lagoona toppled over.

Gil, Mr. Blue, and all the kids leaped up and headed toward the stage. The ghouls raced toward their stricken friend.

Lagoona never hit the stage. Everyone who loved her caught her.

The crowd was giggling uncomfortably. Was this part of the dance routine? Was it supposed to be funny—or moving? They didn't know how to react.

Gil stepped center stage and held up his hand. "Hey! Stop it! Quiet!" he ordered. "You know what? Out of everyfish here, I've actually seen this ghoul dance. And she's fintastic. You don't know what you're missing out on!"

Toralei joined Gil. "Lagoona wanted to conquer her fear and come dance for you again, so she did the most courageous thing I've ever seen anyfish do."

"She went to the Dark and faced the Kraken," Clawdeen told everyone. "The horrible and disgusting beast of the deep."

The crowd gasped in disbelief.

Kala's four hands were balled up in fists. She was furious.

Frankie ignored her. "Then Lagoona came up here," she explained, "and faced you all. Even though she was scared, even though she knew there was a chance she'd go belly up, she swam out onstage and tried."

"And that's more beautiful than any dance you're going to see here tonight," added Draculaura.

Toralei nodded. "So maybe sometime you should

try clapping instead of laughing, and you might see something beautiful too."

The ghouls looked at Toralei in disbelief. She had changed a lot in just a couple of days.

The audience was so quiet you could hear a bubble pop. It was as if everyone was holding his or her breath, waiting to see what might happen. At last, Lagoona blinked. She looked around. But this time she didn't see the audience—she saw her family and friends surrounding her.

"Besides," added Toralei, "I'm the only one who gets to be mean to Lagoona." She winked and Lagoona smiled, accepting the cat's apology.

"Let's get out of here," suggested Gil.

They all swam backstage, still holding on to Lagoona. The audience applauded.

The emcee announced the next act. "I give you Kala Mer'ri and the Krew!" he exclaimed.

Kala took the stage ready to dance, but the audience was still cheering for Lagoona. Kala was even more furious, if that was possible.

"Quiet!" she shouted. "I'm queen of the reef."

But the audience wasn't listening to her. "Lagoona Blue! Lagoona Blue! Lagoona Blue!"

"She's a fluke!" raged Kala. "This is my time! I'm ready to dance!"

But nobody was listening. Mr. Blue handed Lagoona a bouquet of flowers.

Kala was screaming. "No! Stop!"

Toralei pulled out her iCoffin. She was recording Kala's temper tantrum.

"I'm ready to start!" Kala fumed. "You are always trying to keep me out. You are all trying to keep me out."

Lagoona was listening to her, puzzled. "What are you talking about? No one's trying to keep you out."

"Don't worry," said Mr. Blue. "We're leaving right now."

"Don't talk to me! You're not my father!" yelled Kala. Kala crouched down onstage. What was she doing? The crowd watched, fascinated.

Kala stood up at last. She stretched her arms up toward the surface of the ocean and the faraway sky.

She opened her mouth, and what came out of it was a sound that no one had ever heard before. Like a tsunami's roar, like the bellow of a humpback whale, like one very angry teenage sea monster.

Everyone covered his or her ears.

"What's she doing?" wondered Draculaura.

"I don't know," Frankie answered.

"Nothing good, I bet," noted Clawdeen.

The ground beneath them started trembling. The amphitheater started shaking. The stage wobbled. The waters grew darker and darker.

"The Kraken," realized Lagoona.

The crowd freaked out. They abandoned their seats and ran toward the exits. A giant tentacle slipped over the edge of the amphitheater. The Kraken was going to get them all.

"Run!" screamed Lagoona.

Chaos ruled. The Kraken was ripping the amphitheater apart with his tentacles. He flung chunks of the building here and there. Gil wrapped his manta ray wings around the little ones to protect them from falling debris. Mr. Blue, frantically looking for them, was relieved to see them safe with Gil.

"I think these belong to you, Mr. Blue," Gil said, turning them over to their father. "Later, squids."

Gil caught up with the ghouls. They were all trying to keep from getting hit by pieces of the amphitheater. A huge rock was about to smash into Clawdeen when Toralei jumped in front of her. She used her spikes to spear it before it hit her. "Catlike reflexes," Toralei bragged.

The ghouls swam to safety. But Pearl and Peri were not so lucky. Their single tail got caught underneath a piece of debris. They couldn't get loose! The Kraken was coming for them. Kala swam by.

"Help, Kala!" they cried.

"Sorry, ghouls," Kala said dismissively. "If you can't keep up, you get left behind."

Peri and Pearl were trapped. "She left us," moaned Pearl. "I can't believe it. Now what do we do?"

"C'mon, sis," Peri urged. "We can do this. We don't need Kala. We have each other."

"You're right," realized Pearl at last. "We can get out of this mess. We just have to put our…back into it!"

Working together, they pulled themselves out from under the debris. They high-fived each other. "Woo-hoo!" hollered Pearl. They were free but not out of danger.

The Kraken was on the loose.

Chapter 18

TENTACLES!

The Kraken and Kala were chasing the ghouls through town.

"What now?" wondered Clawdeen.

"We need to lead the Kraken away from everyone," Lagoona explained, still swimming. She was racing toward Posea's garden as fast as she could.

"Posea, help!" gasped Draculaura with her last breath when they reached the beautiful flowers of coral and kelp.

Posea was listening to music on a shell-shaped iCoffin, tending to her plants. She couldn't hear a thing. She had no idea what was happening. "*Love is like a storm*," she warbled along with the song she was listening to.

"The Kraken is coming!" yelled Gil, trying to get her attention.

The Sea Mares began chattering right in front of Posea, making all kinds of signs and hand signals. It looked like they had drawn a skull and crossbones in the water, and then a tentacled Kraken. Posea whirled around.

"Lagoona!" she exclaimed. "Did you face your fear?"

"Yes!" Lagoona answered.

"Oh, good." Posea smiled, but her mouth dropped when she looked at Lagoona's plant. "Oh no, no, no. Something is still not right. Your sea lifeline is still… Well, look."

Lagoona couldn't believe it. "But…"

A huge current of water blasted through the

garden. The Kraken was getting closer. He roared and bellowed, sending huge vibrations through the water.

"Really fun talking to you," Lagoona said as fast as she could, "but right now we've got a Kraken problem. Send us back to Monster High!"

Posea did not look alarmed. "You know, if you go back now, your fear will only follow you."

"I'm begging you!" Lagoona pleaded.

Posea was put out. "This is so breaking the rules."

"Please!" demanded Lagoona.

"*So be it*!" Posea went full goddess as she issued her command. She raised her arms, casting some kind of spell in the Kraken's direction. A whirlpool began churning. It sucked up the ghouls in its vortex away from the garden. Up, up, up they rose. Higher and higher. The water changed color, becoming bluer, fresher, and chlorinated. They were back in the pool at Monster High!

Ghoulia, Clawd, Cleo, and Abbey had been checking in regularly at the pool for the last couple of days, hoping their friends would show up. Where had they gone? When would they come back?

Meowlody and Purrsephone, Toralei's werecat friends, were sunbathing.

"So nice to be able to talk now that Toralei's gone," purred Meowlody.

"Yeah," Purrsephone agreed. "She always hogs the conversation."

A bubble burbled in the pool. *Blurp. Blurp. Blurp.* The bubbles were bigger. There were more and more of them. All of a sudden a geyser of water burst up into the air. The ghouls and Gil rode on top of it! They screamed as they sailed through the air. The water drenched Meowlody and Purrsephone. They were completely soaked and yowling.

Gil landed in a tree. Toralei landed on Clawdeen.

"I thought cats always landed on their feet," grumbled Clawdeen.

"Hey," hissed Toralei, "I'd like to see you land on…" She looked down, startled. "Wait! I have feet!"

Sure enough, all the ghouls and Gil too were back to their original selves. They weren't fishified anymore.

"I have my legs back!" exclaimed Draculaura. "It's a good thing. I like my shoes!"

Posea's spell was broken.

"Is everyone okay?" asked Frankie.

Lagoona breathed a sigh of relief. "We made it! It's over!"

But she had spoken too soon.

The surface of the pool was rippling and darkening. The water was shivering. Another geyser burst up and up—and on top of this one? Kala! She was riding the Kraken!

Clawdeen gulped in terror. "I don't know when we are gonna learn to stop saying things like that."

Kala was riding the Kraken like a bronco. Her arms were wrapped around his giant head and she held on expertly as he lurched and bolted.

"Well, well, well!" she shouted, looking around. "Looks like running away to Monster High didn't work this time.

"Destroy it all!" boomed Kala. "Starting with her!" She pointed directly at Lagoona.

"Swim!" shouted Lagoona. "I mean, RUN!"

Chapter 19

REELING IN KALA

Lagoona, Gil, and the ghouls raced into the high school.

"Let's split up," suggested Lagoona. "They can't catch all of us."

Frankie and Draculaura ran one way while Gil, Clawdeen, and Lagoona ran the other. The Kraken's giant eye peered through the front door.

"Come out, come out, wherever you are," Kala called. The Kraken's tentacles ripped down walls and began slithering through the hallways.

In one of the classrooms, the monsters were focused on taking a test. "Hey," said Jackson Jekyll, noticing the giant head of the Kraken. "Eyes on your own paper."

A wall crumbled. A tentacle probed. A moment later, the whole class ran screaming out of the room. The Kraken swiped at them with a long, slimy arm.

Frankie and Draculaura ran into the Creepateria and found Heath and Clawd. Clawd was digging into his lunch—a big steak.

Draculaura couldn't believe it. "Clawd Wolf! Drop that steak!" shouted the vegetarian vampire.

Clawd was busted. "Draculaura! You're back."

Draculaura wrapped her arms around him in a big hug—and tipped his plate onto the floor at the same time.

"The school is under attack!" she told him.

"We need everyone's help to fight," Frankie explained.

"What fight?"

"Fight who?"

The boys were completely confused.

"That!" shouted Frankie. Kala stood at the entrance to the Creepateria.

"WHERE. IS. LAGOONA?" she demanded.

Heath shrugged. "She doesn't look so tough."

"Not that," gasped Draculaura. "That!"

The Kraken crashed through the walls. His giant eyes scanned the room for Lagoona.

"Now that looks *too* tough!" decided Clawd.

Without another word, they all took off out the other door.

Everyone was headed to the Vampitheater. Lagoona jumped onstage and ducked behind the curtain, while the others followed her.

They took a moment to catch their breaths. "What are we going to do?" wondered Draculaura.

"We can't destroy him," Gil noted.

"We can't outrun him," stated Clawdeen.

"The Kraken is going to destroy Monster High and there's nothing we can do about it!" Frankie cried.

Draculaura was trying to figure something out. "Wherever Kala is, the Kraken isn't far behind," she realized.

"It's like she controls him," replied Frankie.

"That's why I need you to distract the Kraken for me," Lagoona announced.

"What's your plan?" asked Clawdeen.

"We can't beat them and we can't outrun them. The only chance we have of saving Monster High is for me to persuade Kala to call off the Kraken," explained Lagoona.

"True dat," Clawdeen agreed.

"Do you think you can do that?" Draculaura asked.

"I have to," said Lagoona, resolved. "But I'll need a distraction."

The ghouls were sure they could do it. They just had to make sure the Kraken didn't catch them while they lured him away.

They waited, listening. They could hear the plopping sound of the Kraken's suction cups sticking and un-sticking along the hallway. A moment later, Kala burst into the Vampitheater and strode down an aisle toward the stage. The Kraken's giant eye filled the doorway.

"I hope you're all ready for a little stage *fright*!" Kala called out, giggling. The Kraken crashed into the Vampitheater.

"I don't like this plan," murmured Clawdeen.

"It's the only one we've got!" said Lagoona.

Abbey was the only one who didn't seem upset. "Yeti afraid of nothing but yak milk shortage. Let's with the doing."

"We're in," said Frankie bravely.

"Operation Kraken Distraction!" announced Draculaura.

"Roar!" growled Toralei. "Let's do it!"

Everyone nodded.

"Oh, Lagoona!" Kala called with fake sweetness. "I know you're in there. Did you freeze onstage again?"

Kala stalked onto the stage and tore apart the theater curtains. The stage was empty. The monsters had escaped!

She let out a frustrated scream and commanded the Kraken to find them. The Kraken burst through the walls of Monster High and slithered down the exterior and onto the school grounds.

But the monsters were ready to create a distraction. "No, Lagoona!" they shouted. "Don't go that way. The Kraken's out here!"

Lagoona and Gil jumped out of the bushes and waved their hands. "Hey! Kraken!"

Kala pointed at Lagoona, directing the Kraken. "Over there!"

The Kraken lunged toward Lagoona, but Abbey froze the ground under his tentacles. He slipped and fell.

"Let's put this stinky fish on ice!" Abbey suggested gleefully.

"Who's freezing now, Kala?" taunted Clawdeen.

Somehow the Kraken managed to clamber back up on his tentacles. Kala jumped on his back.

"Deuce, that's your cue!" directed Clawdeen.

Deuce, the snake-haired gorgon, took off his dark glasses. Without them, his eyes were all-powerful, turning everything he looked at into stone. "Hey, Kraken-a-laken," he called. "Eyes on me, dude!"

Gil saw a tentacle curling around behind Deuce. "Look out!" he screamed.

The Kraken swiped the ground where Deuce and

119

Abbey stood, covering them in a mound of dirt.

"Harsh!" came the muffled voice of Deuce.

Abbey clawed her way out from under the dirt pile. "Ptooey," she spat. "Never to be sending a gorgon to do a job of the Yeti."

"Where's Lagoona?" demanded Kala from the top of the Kraken.

"Hey, Mr. Kraken," Frankie called. "Over here!"

"LAGOONA!" shouted Kala. "SHOW YOURSELF!"

Lagoona and Clawdeen took off. The Kraken raced after them.

Toralei bravely jumped in front of the Kraken. "Hey, fish head," she taunted him. "Watch this! Drop me a beat."

Meowlody and Purrsephone hit play on the boom box from their dance practices. "Consider the beat dropped."

Toralei let loose with a wild, jerking dance routine. "Something nobody has the power to look away from," she sang. "JAZZ HANDS!" She flared her fingers, wiggling and stomping.

The Kraken looked baffled. He blinked his big eyes. He stared. He stopped blinking. He didn't move. He was distracted!

Meanwhile, Lagoona had managed to run behind the Kraken, and she was climbing up his slippery body toward the roof—where Kala was. "Kala!" she whispered when she was just a few feet away from her.

Kala whirled around, stunned.

"Please call off the Kraken," Lagoona asked.

Kala's eyes narrowed. "You can't always run from what scares you."

"No, Kala," agreed Lagoona. "I ran to it. To you."

Kala was confused. "You're afraid of...*me*?"

"Of course I am!" Lagoona admitted. "You bullied me!"

"Maybe that's because the entire town bullied me," Kala shot back.

Now it was Lagoona's turn to be surprised. What was Kala talking about? Lagoona was genuinely confused. "I don't understand."

"Of course you don't. No one does." There were tears in Kala's eyes.

"But I want to," said Lagoona, reaching out to her long-ago friend. "Just please, call off the Kraken."

Draculaura was running toward the Kraken on one side, and Frankie was charging at him from the other.

"Over here!" they both called at the same moment.

The Kraken whirled around, swiping with all his tentacles. He roared and bellowed. In their terror, Draculaura and Frankie careened into each other. The Kraken looked up. He saw Lagoona and Kala on the roof.

"It's terrible, isn't it?" Kala hissed at Lagoona. "To see the people you love being chased away in fear."

"Why are you doing this?" asked Lagoona. She needed to know.

"You'll never understand what it's like for someone to hate you for what you are! To not give you a chance because of what you look like. To hide you away because you scare them."

Lagoona didn't understand. "Who's done that to you?"

"Everyone!" screamed Kala.

As she shouted, a giant tentacle curled over the rim of the roof and wrapped itself tightly around Lagoona. She was trapped by the Kraken! He had her!

"But you are destroying a place that doesn't do that." Lagoona had to get through to Kala. She just had to. "Monster High is different."

The Kraken was beginning to squeeze her tight like a boa constrictor.

The monsters, looking up, were stricken with horror.

But Lagoona somehow kept her cool. "No one is an outcast here," she told Kala.

"I don't believe you."

"It's true!" Lagoona persisted. "At Monster High we accept everybody's freaky flaws—scary or spooky, ghost or goblin, vampire or werewolf. There's a place for every monster!"

All of a sudden, Lagoona realized something for the first time. There was even a place for *her* at Monster High, a sea monster with stage fright. "At Monster High we accept everybody as they are."

Kala looked down beneath her. There were so many different kinds of monsters here—not just sea creatures. There were mummies and werewolves and voodoo dolls. There were ghosts and vampires and ghouls. And they were all trying to save their friend Lagoona. All these different monsters were getting along with one another.

Kala wanted to be accepted. She really did. She didn't want to be an outcast forever.

The Kraken was squeezing Lagoona even tighter. It was harder and harder for her to speak. "Take me if you have to," she told him. "But leave Monster High alone."

Kala held up her hand, thinking. "So here, at Monster High...I won't be judged for my flaws?"

"Never!" squeaked Lagoona.

Kala nodded. "Put her down, Dad."

The Kraken unwound his tentacle and placed Lagoona back on the roof. Everyone was watching. No one could take in what they had seen—and heard.

"Dad??" asked Lagoona, stunned.

"Dad?" repeated all the monsters.

Kala looked ashamed. She had revealed her big secret. At last. But maybe this was too much of a flaw, even for Monster High. She took a breath.

"Dad," she began shyly.

The great eyes of the Kraken blinked.

"Dad, this is my childhood friend, Lagoona. Lagoona, this is my dad."

Chapter 20

THE COAST IS CLEAR

The Kraken helped the monsters repair Monster High. Kala's dad lifted stones and repaired walls. Lagoona helped wipe down the lockers covered in sea slime. Kala squeegeed the floors using her tail.

Clawdeen added some soap to a bucket. "So," she said to Kala, "the Kraken is your dad?"

"And that stuff we saw in the Dark," said Lagoona. "That was yours?"

Kala nodded. "My bedroom."

Frankie remembered something. "The pictures on the rock!"

"Dad's drawings of me." Kala blushed.

Later on, when Kala and Lagoona were repairing

the staircase brick by brick, Lagoona asked Kala another question that had been on her mind. "So when Peri told me you had looked the Kraken in the eye..."

"I look him in the eye all the time." Kala shrugged. "He's my dad. I go down every weekend to visit."

"But the rest of the town..." Lagoona's voice trailed off as she remembered all the things she'd heard residents of the Great Scarrier Reef say about the Kraken.

"The rest of the town thought he was evil," said Kala. "Just beclaws of his looks."

Lagoona placed one brick on top of another. She was remembering something she had said long, long ago to Kala.

Just before they had gone onstage together, Lagoona had said something terrible to her. "Kala," Lagoona remembered her twelve-year-old self saying, "you're as clumsy as a kraken. But even the big ol' Kraken could do this step. The Kraken is slimy and disgusting. The evil Kraken eats bad little children. Krakens are so slimy and disgusting. Careful! Or the ugly, horrible Kraken will get you."

Lagoona felt very, very sad. "Including me," she admitted to Kala.

"They ran away every time they saw him," Kala

confided. "So one day I ran away too."

"Oh, Kala!" It broke Lagoona's heart to hear this.

"I was ashamed that he was my dad."

"I'm so sorry."

Kala sighed. "When I saw you with your big, happy family, the kind of family that no one ran away from, I was so angry. It took a long time for me to see and accept him as he really is. But it's really my fault. If I had told people, if I had explained, if I had shown them that my dad just looks scary…"

"It's okay," said Lagoona.

"They didn't know that he taught me how to roller surf. And that he makes an amazing kelpburger."

Lagoona smiled. "Well, I do now."

Lagoona and Kala continued working on rebuilding the steps—and their friendship.

"You'd really like him," Kala told Lagoona. "If you got to know him. Everyone would."

Suddenly Lagoona had a great idea. "Then you should join us here! I told you, we accept everyone's freaky flaws. And their scary dads!"

Kala beamed. "I'm so sorry I made fun of you for going belly up."

"The past made me who I am today, even the scary stuff," Lagoona admitted. "And I like who I am. Freaky flaws and all."

Shyly, Kala held out her hand in a gesture of peace and forgiveness. But Lagoona pulled her into a hug. The past was behind them and they were friends again.

Not only had Lagoona faced her deepest fear—she had made friends with her!

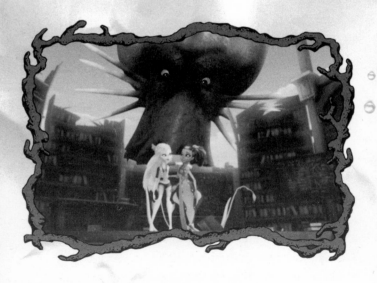

Chapter 21

POOL PARTY

Repairing the school brought everyone together. Mr. Kraken did all the heavy lifting, of course, and he turned out, underneath his gruesome appearance, to just be a big teddy bear. With tentacles. Long tentacles covered in suction cups. Things aren't always what they seem.

The Kraken gently lifted monsters up to their ladders where they painted, and he helped Lagoona's brothers and sisters get to the top of the slide at the pool. He was looking out for everyone.

Once they were all done with their work, Lagoona decided to throw a great big pool party. Her dad was in charge of refreshments.

"This burger's choice, mate," said Mr. Blue to her friends. "Best burgers ever. These kelpburgers are yummo!"

Gil came over to Lagoona and smiled happily. They looked into each other's eyes. Not only had Gil finally met her family, but she had discovered just how much he cared about her. What would she have done without him?

The Kraken draped himself around the pool so ghouls and mansters could slide down his tentacles like giant waterslides.

When Toralei arrived at the party, Lagoona rushed over to her.

"So," purred Toralei. "Am I invited to *this* party?"

"Of course!" reassured Lagoona. "Everymonster is."

Kala emerged from the swimming pool.

"*Everymonster* everymonster?" she asked.

"Sure!" exclaimed Frankie.

"C'mon on up, ghouls!" Kala shouted.

The two heads of Pearl and Peri bobbed to the surface. They looked around, wide-eyed. They'd never seen land before!

"Welcome to Monster High!" said Draculaura with a wide smile.

Kala helped them out of the pool. "Come on, ghouls. Join the party.

"I like the new Kala," Peri whispered to Pearl.

"She's so nice to us now!" her sister agreed.

"But it's bizarre up here," said Peri. "Nothing is floating. It's like everything is anchored."

"This place is boo-tiful," Pearl noted. "But it's really dry!"

Toralei covered her ears and snarled. "I don't know if two heads are better than one, but they sure yap twice as much!"

Clawdeen laughed to see Toralei so put out. "Okay, now I know everything's back to normal."

Clawdeen noticed that Lagoona was tacking up a new poster. BE YOURSELF! BE UNIQUE! BE A MONSTER! On it was a photograph of Lagoona—going belly up. If she could get up onstage, anyone could!

Chapter 22

SEA STAR

Far away under the sea, Posea was swimming around her garden tending her ocean flowers. The Sea Mares scampered around her like little sea horses, sending columns of bubbles through the water.

Posea stopped when she came to Lagoona's special plant. It was bursting with vitality, sending long blue and green tendrils out into the sea that wafted back and forth in the tidal currents. Lagoona was clearly better than she had ever been—healthier and happier.

"Ahh, much better." Posea smiled.

Beside Lagoona's sea lifeline was a strange aquatic plant. It was like a squid had been crossed with a cactus. It too looked very healthy and happy.

It belonged to Kala, and Posea had never seen it looking better.

She gave it a spritz of fertilizer.

She liked being a sea goddess—and she really was getting better at it. She was.

MONSTER HIGH

BOO YORK, BOO YORK
A MONSTERRIFIC MUSICAL!™

TAXI

Turn the page for a sneak peek at another creeperific story!

CHAPTER 1

The Purr-fect Pop Star

The skyline of Boo York shone in the darkness. Lights blazed from the Monster of Liberty's torch, the top of the Vampire State Building, the golden Ptolemy Tower, and the flashing neon signs of Times Scare. But the brightest light of all was a fiery comet shooting across the sky.

From inside a packed theater on Bloodway, a spotlight revealed Catty Noir opening her mouth onstage to sing her hit ballad, "Love Is a Storm." The crowd cheered. Cameras clicked. The stage lit up with pyrotechnic fires, illuminating a backdrop of diamond-like pieces of broken mirrors. Catty's pink mane of hair, the same color as her sequined gown, fell to her waist in long, soft curls. Her dark eyes were full of soul. Pure, pitch-perfect notes filled the arena of Madison Scare Garden. No wonder Catty Noir was an international pop sensation and *Thrillboard* magazine's musician of the century. She could sing about love like no other monster.

"*Love is like a storm tonight. Love in the air, love in the clouds, love like a flood!*"

As her voice hit the last note, the crowd began to clap and cheer. Catty bowed and blew kisses to the audience. "Thank you! I love you, Boo York! Good-bye!" After the curtain came down, Catty slipped out of the back of the theater and headed to her waiting limo. Black-suited security gargoyles kept back the crowds as fans thrust programs and autograph books toward her to sign. Catty tried to smile, but she was overwhelmed by the glare of her success. As the door shut behind her, Catty closed her eyes. She was exhausted.

The next day, *Thrillboard* magazine's cover story was about Catty. But it wasn't about the concert—the big news was that Catty, the queen of the love song, was dropping out of show business! But why? No one knew…except Catty.